KATHERINE BLESSAN

T for Tolerance

To Jodie
Hope you enjoy it!
lots of love

x x

Aug 2023

Contents

Chapter 1   1
Chapter 2   10
Chapter 3   17
Chapter 4   26
Chapter 5   32
Chapter 6   39
Chapter 7   46
Chapter 8   53
Chapter 9   59
Chapter 10   63
Chapter 11   71
Chapter 12   79
Chapter 13   87
Chapter 14   94
Chapter 15   106
Chapter 16   118
Chapter 17   125
Chapter 18   132
Chapter 19   139
Chapter 20   148
Chapter 21   156
Chapter 22   162
Chapter 23   171
Chapter 24   178

Chapter 25   185
Chapter 26   190
Chapter 27   198
Acknowledgements   213
Other books by Katherine Blessan   215

Chapter 1

Truth is dangerous. Society has taught me that and I'm still learning today, painstakingly walking the jagged edge of this knowledge. They won't tell you this in so many words, but it's hard-wired into our thinking. Tolerance, tolerance, tolerance. But you're only seen as tolerant when you believe the 'right thing'. And I don't, apparently.

November 8th, 2040. It's one of those wet, blustery autumn days when, no matter what I do, my hair ends up all twisty and frizzy. Naomi's raven hair always looks so sleek, like her straighteners have had a permanent locking in effect. It's hard to believe we're from the same gene pool, let alone twins. We trudge up the hill from the school, measuring our breath with the pounding of our feet. We live barely five minutes away from the school so can hardly complain, but it's one of the steepest hills in the whole of Sheffield and I always feel like I've had a good workout when I get home.

Our house is perched on the hilltop like an eagle's eyrie. It's an old five bed Victorian detached, and we're blessed by several birches waving over our garden wall, providing us with shade and comfort. Whenever Mum grumbles about soggy leaves being dragged all over the house, Dad reminds us that we're lucky we didn't lose our trees in the tree felling scandal of thirty or so years ago.

Naomi powers up on my right side and jostles me to the front door.

Irritation flickers up my spine. "Do you have to act like a five-year-old?" I throw out.

"What do you mean?" she asks, giving me a wide-eyed look.

I narrow my eyes. "Always trying to beat me. So juvenile."

Whistling tunelessly, she ignores me and holds her hand up to the door sensor until it flashes green and clicks open. Although Naomi's my closest buddy, she's like Sellotape folded sticky side out; you just can't pry her from your fingers.

The Hudson-home smell of polished floors mingled with gardenia reed diffuser greets me. I shuffle out of my shoes and push past the coats at the entrance into the wide, echoey hallway. Behind me, Naomi takes off her shoes and places them with precision on the shoe rack.

"Fancy a smoothie?" I ask.

"Ooh, yes please," says Naomi, her face crinkling into a grin. I make a mean smoothie if I say so myself.

After tossing frozen mangoes and chopped up bananas into the mixer, I scoop out a few dollops of Greek yogurt, pour in some Nutella flavoured milkshake and a handful of chia seeds to finish. Naomi takes out two glass tumblers from a kitchen cupboard and watches me, her almond-shaped eyes narrowing slightly like they always do when she's thinking.

I flick on the mixer and the ingredients whirl together, creating a faint humming noise throughout the room.

"Sathya?"

"Mmmhuh," I say, switching off the machine and pouring the smoothie into the tumblers.

2

"I keep thinking about what Mr Baldwick said about the Christian faith today."

I use my fingertip to wipe off a smidgeon of smoothie from the edge of the tumbler and pop it into my mouth. "Don't worry, I'll have this one," I say, smiling at Naomi, knowing how she feels about germs.

For once, she doesn't comment on my hygiene. "I'd never thought of it this way before, but isn't it a hateful thing to say that no one can get to heaven except through Jesus? Doesn't it limit God's love to a chosen few?"

"I don't think it's hateful at all," I utter, though a ripple runs through my guts. If Naomi has doubts, I'd feel much better if we sorted them out together. "God wants everyone to know him, but not everyone chooses him. Look – you don't have to believe everything that our teachers say. You can think for yourself."

"I am. That's exactly what I'm doing." Naomi frowns and sips on her smoothie.

"We're a minority now – in the UK at least. Don't minorities deserve respect in this supposedly tolerant state?"

"He wasn't saying that we aren't respected," she responds. "He's asking us to think about whether our views are respectful of others."

I snort. Maybe not the most sensitive of responses, but sometimes all this political correctness gets right up my nose. "What could possibly be more respectful and loving than 'do to others as you would have done to you' and 'love your enemies as yourself'? Honestly, Naomi."

"Don't be like that, Sathya, I'm just working things out for myself." She twists her body away from the kitchen counter and walks off, carrying the rest of her smoothie. I can tell by

3

the tilt of her shoulders that she's in a huff.

Rather than calling for her to come back or apologizing for my smugness, I decide to head up to my room and get started on homework. There's plenty of time for us to iron out our differences.

My screen lights up as I slide my tablet onto my lap. I have every intention of getting started with my political studies. The Newman Academy gave up on doing traditional A-levels four years back. We now do the IB Diploma, which fits better with the internationalist, liberal mindset that our school wants to pursue. A-levels have fallen out of fashion these days, encouraged by the fact that the top global universities favour the IB.

I keep thinking about what Mr Baldwick and Naomi said, and decide I'll just have five minutes on Mandoo thrashing out my thoughts with my believing peer group. Picking up my phone, I snap a picture of my tablet to show that I'm serious about getting to work. Flicking my finger above my screen in time with my thoughts, I write, *I'm going to start my homework soon, LOL!* then I hammer out my thoughts about faith, Jesus and political correctness and finish with a passionate flourish – *Jesus really IS the only way, and I don't care what the thought police say.*

A minute later, *You go girl!* flashes up on my screen and a smile sinks through me. Trust Taila to be my one-woman fan club. I turn off my phone Wi-Fi and toss it onto my bed.

Now that I've got it out of my system, I can concentrate on Marxism and Socialism for the rest of the evening. A good hour or so, anyway. Mum will be home soon. She mentioned she was going to make masala dosa this evening – my favourite.

I'm so engrossed in the thinking of world changers like

Malala Yousafzai and Greta Thunberg, that I don't notice Mum pad into the room behind me in stockinged feet. A cool hand on my exposed shoulder makes me jump and I turn around, heart thumping. "Mum! You scared the flip out of me! Couldn't you have given me some sort of advance warning?"

Mum raises her dark eyebrows up at me and rocks her head from side to side. "Sathya, I'm hardly the devil," she says in her South Indian lilt. "What do I need to warn you for?" She gives me a rebuking tap on my upper arm. "I thought you might like to know that dinner's ready. Naomi's already downstairs."

"What about Dad?" I say, following Mum downstairs, grateful for food and family and my productive study hour.

"He's been working from home all day, but he's taking an important holographic call right now, so he said not to wait for him."

"That's not like you, Mum. You always wait for Dad," I say, tucking my hand in hers, childlike, as we enter the kitchen-diner.

"Tschk. I know, but my stomach is playing up, and it's harder for me to eat late these days."

Naomi blinks at us after placing the finishing touches to the dinner table and chews her bottom lip. She has the bad habit of doing that when something is playing on her mind. When we were waiting for our MYP results last year, Naomi chewed her lip so much that it bled. Of course, she had top grades in every subject, but trust her to be worried that she would do badly.

Mum and I sit down at the table next to Naomi and we hold our hands around the table. Mum is Hindu and Dad has no faith affiliation, but this habit of giving thanks for the good things in life has been a part of our family culture since I can remember. The rest of us thank God, but Dad just thanks the universe or whatever you do as a secularist. Rubbing her stomach with one hand, Mum winces and says, "Thank God for a productive day and for the rain."

Naomi looks pointedly at me, and says, "Thank God for sweet Sathya."

A fishlike shiver courses through me. I can't quite tell if she means it as a compliment or as a subtle jab at me to be nicer. Naomi and Mum are looking at me, waiting for my response, and I stutter out a thanksgiving without giving it much thought.

"Thank God for school, family and dead leaves!" I clear my throat and it turns into a little laugh.

"Dead leaves?" Naomi raises her eyebrows, then gives a spluttering sound, which sounds like a strangled frog.

Mum expertly slides the thin, crispy dosa onto our plates. She has perfected her technique so that they melt in your mouth like the South Indian restaurants. I scoop some sambar curry and dollop it onto my dosa, then pass the bowl to Mum. From the other side of the table, Naomi hands me the bowl of coconut chutney. The key with Keralan cuisine is the mixing of the flavours and the tart spiciness of the sambar, mixed with the coconut and ghee in the dosa never fails to stir my tastebuds.

"Hey, what's all this? Eating without me!" Dad's voice booms good humouredly as he enters the room.

"Please, join us, Ant," says Mum. She stands up to serve Dad. She has the habit of doing that – it's a cultural thing.

"Sit down, please, Vidhya," Dad murmurs, putting a gentle pressure onto her hands. "I'll help myself."

This little interaction plays out frequently at our dinner table; it's not just role playing, but a genuine expression of what's important to them – Mum has it built into her to serve, and Dad has it built into him to be self-sufficient.

"My meeting finished earlier than I expected. Mayeso was easier to get onside than I thought he'd be." Rapidly piling his plate with food, Dad widens his eyes, pushes back his wild salt and pepper hair with one hand, then tucks in.

"What did you get him onside with?" I ask, swallowing a mouthful of food.

Shaking his head lightly, Dad replies, "It's confidential, sweetpea, sorry." It's Dad's pet-name for me. Naomi is nimbycheeks, which is far more embarrassing. Thankfully, he doesn't use these names outside the home. I would curl up like a hedgehog and die if he did.

"Why bring it up if you're not going to tell the whole story? It's so annoying."

Dad smiles ruefully. "Mum knows what I'm talking about, and it just so happens that she's in the room too."

Dad is a business consultant, which means he's called upon by all sorts of important people to help them out with tricky business problems. Mayeso is his business partner and the father of my best friend – Taila.

It's 8pm by the time we've finished eating, talking and clearing up. I take my phone and curl up on the sofa in the lounge, ready for some screen chat. Dad has gone up to the office for yet another meeting, and Mum is with me in the lounge, reading a book and listening to music through headphones. Naomi has headed up to her room.

Humming to myself, I click on the Mandoo app, ready to engage in the discussion stirred up by my thought splurge earlier. Yet instead of entering, a black box pops up with an error message. Tricksy techno problems don't phase me – normally. I click off the app, wait a few seconds, then try again. Same problem. The AI troubleshooter can't fix it, even after a

7

few seconds. I sigh.

"Everything ok?" Mum asks, looking up from her book.

"Yes, I'm having some minor app problems, but I can sort it."

I slump back into my seat and try another app – Twitter. It's the same problem. Then I try Snapchat, which I use less of these days, and the same enigmatic black screen comes up on my phone. I can't even get into my email account! Dread rises within me. This is not a normal technical problem.

"I'm just going up to my room," I say, giving Mum a nudge on the knee. Even though she's an intelligent woman, I wouldn't even know how to begin talking to her about the problem. It'll have to be Naomi.

Naomi's room is opposite mine. Her door is ajar and the rhythmic beat of music from retro indie band Slipstream spills out onto the landing. The words of 'Psycho Paul' are sung with slurry intensity to a funky melody. I knock on the door. She's a bit less precious about her privacy than I am, but I wouldn't want anyone to just walk in on me, so I don't do it to her. I watch her shadow distort on the carpet as she moves across the room from her bed.

"Hey," she says, opening the door to me. "What's happening?"

I come in and close the door behind me. Something tells me it's wise to do that. Her room is immaculately tidy, unlike mine. Every book is lined up on her shelf in size and genre order. The inside of her wardrobe is organized by category and size, unlike my messy hodgepodge of worn clothes and shoes gathering cobwebs in the corner. "I've just been trying to get onto my social media accounts, and everything's blocked. Do you know anything about this?"

She settles on the bed, and I plonk myself next to her, shoving my phone in her face.

"Look," I say, showing her first one app and then the next.

"Oh my God," she says, then stares at me aghast. "I can't believe *It's* happened to you, Sathya. What have you been saying?"

"What are you talking about? What's happened to me?"

"Seems like you've been banned – permanently blocked from social media."

"For what?" That feeling like a cold shower washes over me again.

"You tell me..."

I am getting frustrated, my shoulders tightening and my heartbeat rising. "Don't play games with me, Naomi. I'm freaking out right now. If you know, tell me!"

Chapter 2

Three years ago, Naomi and I were on the same page. Dad's only brother, Uncle Pete, had just passed away from bowel cancer. It shook both of us to our cores as you'd expect from fourteen-year-olds who'd never lost anyone close before. I won't forget the night Naomi crept into my bed, her feet cold and her body shaking with grief. We held each other, laughing and crying as we shared anecdotes of Uncle Pete. I doubt we slept over three hours.

"Where do you think he is now?" Naomi asked, and that set us both on a journey of exploration, seeking answers, seeking truth. Dad told us that his body had simply gone into the ground, back to the soil from which it came, and that we should be thankful for the life he'd lived. Mum said she believed his soul would be reincarnated into another body and that since he'd been a good man, he'd have a good next life. Our parents' differing beliefs kept us open-minded, yet neither of us felt fully convinced by their answers.

Taila Masemi was the one who first got me thinking about Jesus. Taila is of Zambian heritage and has had a strong, rich faith ever since I've known her. As soon as she stepped into Ms Daimler's classroom nine years ago and sat next to me on the desk I shared with three others, we connected over our love of sports and our shared humour. I couldn't help noticing she was wearing the same black and white platform trainers as I was. We tapped our toes together under the desk, then I linked her little finger with mine and we looked at each other and smiled. That was it – bonded for life.

After Uncle Pete died, I couldn't help noticing how Taila stepped up to support me. She'd always been a close friend, but now I could contact her at any time of day, and she was always there for me. She opened up to me about how tough it was for her when her mother had died before moving to England, yet despite all that sadness and distress, it was her faith which strengthened her.

Shortly afterwards Taila asked, "Would you be interested in doing a Youth Alpha with me?" She'd mentioned Alpha to me before and I'd always said no, but this time, I thought – well why not? I needed the chance to thrash out my ideas about the meaning of life. Naomi wanted to join in too, so we both did the course. Each session was a holographic meeting, with all the participants beaming in from different locations. Virtual meetings are standard these days – even school is partially virtual, with three days of learning at home and two onsite. It's more efficient and reduces the chance of spreading the highly infectious new viruses, which seem to spring up all over the place these days. Lessons are taught with a mixture of human and AI teacher-bots.

We gradually learned more about genuine Jesus followers – who they are and what they believe and why. The thing that really clinched it for me was listening to Taila's pastor sharing the story of Lazarus – you know, the man who Jesus raised from the dead. Pastor Daniel stood in the middle of the projection circle and enthralled us with a dramatic retelling of the story, making us laugh with the different voices of the characters.

When it came to the part with Martha, there was no more laughing. Daniel stood to one side pretending to be Martha telling Jesus, "If you had been here, my brother would not have died. But even now I know that God will give you whatever you ask." Then Daniel moved position to pretend to be Jesus, and answered, "I am the resurrection and the life. Those who believe in me, even though they die like everyone else, will live again."

At those words, it was like I was suspended in time, the only one there in the room with Daniel. I knew then that it wasn't about physical life or death, but about accepting what Jesus has done and walking joyfully with him. He could choose to bring people back to life again – as he could do anything, but mostly he didn't. The important thing was allowing our lives to be transformed inwardly through accepting his peace and forgiveness. I didn't understand everything then, but it was my moment of 'seeing' for the first time.

Naomi had a similar experience to me and both of us became followers of Jesus (that phrase is more popular among believers than the historical label 'Christians' which has so many negative connotations) in our separate bedrooms that evening. Sheepishly, I went into her room at the end of the meeting and told her about my experience, and she had snot and tears running down her face as she told me that she'd done the same.

The next day, Taila came round to my house before school, looked me in the eye and said, "You did, didn't you?"

"Yeeess," I said, drawing out my vowels. "How did you know?"

"Something in my spirit came alive. It's hard to explain, but I thought – that session did it for Sathya."

"It did for Naomi too," I said, joy bubbling inside.

Taila squealed and squeezed me so hard it hurt my ribs. "I'm so happy!"

"No way. I'd never be able to tell," I said straight-faced, before we gave each other a look of delight and burst into peals of laughter.

Now, Naomi places her tablet on her lap, and we watch some news from a couple of hours ago. It's the Home Secretary, Martin Took, with his shock of red hair pulled back from his forehead like he's permanently startled. I latch onto the words he's saying and allow myself to be dragged across the mental space between me and the rest of the nation listening to him.

"Many of you will be aware of the campaign against hate crime that has rocked our nation over the past couple of decades. Today marks a momentous occasion. New legislation has been implemented making it illegal for anyone to express a thought that could in any way be deemed to be harmful or offensive to another group of people. It will also enshrine in law the value of tolerance. If you express a viewpoint that does not tolerate the views or freedoms of other people, then you will have breached the law and must bear the full consequences of your crime. The result is that certain freedoms must be sacrificed in order to maintain the freedom of others." My head throbs. There are so many unanswered questions in this brief pronouncement, but I can't bear to watch the impassioned media discussion that ensues. I put my hand over the screen, shutting it down.

"I think it's time we tone down our Christian viewpoint," Naomi says solemnly.

"How can you say such a thing?" I am genuinely flabbergasted by Naomi's response.

"This is just the start, Sathya," she says, gripping my hands and eyeballing me. "You've just expressed a strong viewpoint about Jesus being the 'only' way and you've been banned."

"So, you do know what I said in my last Mandoo chat?" I stand up and pace the room, my nerve ends alive.

"Of course, Sathya, I've been part of that same group for as long as you, but I've just kept quiet recently – choosing to observe – and don't like the way things are going."

"How can you say that? You know what, Naomi, it's not us that have changed, it's you. Since when did you become so...?" I shake my head at her.

Naomi grips the bed cover and her knuckles whiten. "Honestly, I'm scared for us! Why can't we express God's love without mentioning any of the things others find offensive?"

"But don't you see? The very centre of our faith – the cross – IS an offense to those rejecting Jesus. If we take that out, we can't say anything! And, if we've got to have some watered-down faith without any substance then I want nothing to do with it."

"Are you aware of what this could mean, Sathya? Are you thinking practically?"

"Practically," I repeat, slumping down on Naomi's bed again. "In what sense?"

Naomi waves her hand over the screen and selects a news tab. "Look. Similar laws have been implemented in Belgium and these are some of the consequences."

"What's the source of this news?" I probe, smug in my knowledge that sources always need to be checked.

"It's an indie news channel run by a Christian media group if you must know."

"Fire away then." I lean forward, cupping my chin in my hands and watch the five-minute video screening on Naomi's cream coloured wall.

Testimonies are being shared – by people with blanked-out faces and distorted voices. It's this that freaks me out most, coming from a so-called free state. A huge muscular guy speaks (with translated English over his native French). "One moment I had a job and was valued for my qualifications and knowledge; then, without warning, I was labelled a 'loose cannon' and dismissed." A petite, well-dressed girl not much older than us tells the interviewer, "I'd been given high predicted grades from my college, but suddenly that no longer mattered. None of the universities wanted me, not a single one." An older woman sitting next to her says, "It's all her wasted talent that bothered me most. I couldn't believe it – still can't." She heaves a shuddering sigh and puts her hand on her daughter's.

After several similar stories, the off-screen interviewer – a Caucasian woman in her mid-30s – appears on camera. "What unites these stories is that they're all outspoken followers of Jesus. They have all publicly declared in one way or another what they believe. We are in a time when Islamophobia has been replaced by Christophobia, yet no one will openly admit this discrimination exists. It's always branded as hate-crime."

As the credits roll and the images vanish, I am silent. Naomi clears her throat and turns to me. "We've got our futures to think about here," she says, her hand on mine clammy.

My head pounds as if my heart is beating in it and I squeeze out my unprocessed thoughts. "Even though that's happening in Belgium, we don't know that the same thing's going to happen here."

"Sathya, you've just been banned for sharing your religious

views. This will not go away!"

"You're right, but..." Stalling for time, I pick up one of Naomi's hair accessories – a crimson bamboo clip shaped like a butterfly – and twirl it between my fingers. The essence of what I want to say bubbles beneath the surface, but I'm struggling to get the words out. "I know that changing what we believe is not the answer. No. I mean – lying about what we believe. There we go – I've said it now."

Naomi blows out her lips in exasperation. "You've always been so outspoken, sweet sis. Maybe now is the time for you just to keep your head down more."

"I'm sorry, Naomi. We're just going to have to agree to disagree on this one."

A gritty nugget, like a rough diamond, settles in me. Stubbornness or an unswerving faith in what's right? Or are they two sides of the same thing?

Chapter 3

Our trainers squeaking against the polished gym floors are the musical accompaniment to our tennis game. Taila's feet leave the ground as she smashes the ball in a smart return shot. I have no chance. I over-reached my backhand and she's won the point – again.

Clenching my jaws, I pass her the ball and let her take the next serve. We rarely have time to play a full match and today is one of those days. We're playing for a set and she's already two games ahead of me. I need to up my game. I know that if I want to beat her, I have to use my cunning – to get Taila to think I'm going to do one thing but do something else instead. After a series of backhand and forehand shots to get back into rhythm, I know that I have to take the advantage quickly otherwise I'm beaten. Using both hands, Taila swings back hard on my forehand, and I see the ball flying towards the centre of the court. Swiftly, I raise my arm back as though I'm going to hit it wide, flick my wrist with a little twist, hit the ball at a different angle from the one Taila's expecting and drop it just over the net.

Wahoo! A point to me. Whooping, I do a little dance on the court.

"Ok. It was a good one," Taila concedes with a grin. She's always a better loser than me, and she's nowhere near losing the set yet.

Within ten minutes, I've powered back into the game, winning the set on a final lob.

Every nerve tingling with elation, we move forward to the edge of the net and give each other a breathless hug. "Thanks for letting me win," I say with a wry grin.

She laughs. "I don't know if I'd go that far! Well done. You deserved it."

Noticing a painful twinge running down my right wrist, I flex my fingers. "Ouch. I think that weird twist I did earlier was not as good for my body as it was for my game."

"Let's go shower up. The heat will help with easing your muscles, hopefully."

We stand outside Ponds Forge near the storage place for bikes and electric scooters. Both of us have electric scooters, which we can use on the vast network of cycle lanes that thread through the city. It's a cold, brisk day at the end of November and the sun is low in the mid-afternoon sky, casting a russet glow over Park Square and on the distinctive flats on the hill beyond. Our hands are snug in our thermogloves. It's been a long time coming, but you can stand near one of the busiest traffic thoroughfares in Sheffield and not be overpowered by scentless but deadly carbon dioxide emissions. I don't remember the worst of it, but our parents tell us how bad it used to be, both here in Sheffield and in Trivandrum where our mother was raised.

"So, that's why you went so quiet on Mandoo," says Taila when I finally get the chance to tell her what's been happening.

I didn't dare tell her on the phone – in case anyone was tapping our conversations – and I'd just evaded her questions. "I thought we'd offended you or something."

"Na. You know me. Not easily offended. I'm telling you – it's been weird but strangely liberating not being able to use social media for two weeks. That compulsion to constantly check what's happening in my world has gone as I've had no other option, and I've noticed things I've not noticed before."

"Like what?"

"Oh – like the incredible details on a spiderweb or the way Dad rubs the back of his neck when he's thinking."

Taila's nod segues into a frown. "Have you thought of telling the police about your banning so that you can use social media again?"

Feeling suddenly protective, I put one hand on Taila's shoulder. She's so innocent. "With the passing of Section 44 of the Public Order Act, the law is not on our side anymore, at least as far as the sharing of our so called 'narrow' beliefs is concerned." I raise my fingers to form speech marks when I say the word narrow. "Naomi tried to get me to reconsider my outspoken views, but I just can't do it."

She scrunches her face and shudders. "I'm surprised I've not been banned too, then. You must have had someone on your case."

"Yeah, maybe," I say. I won't pretend I haven't thought about that possibility, but over the past two weeks I've been trying to focus my mind on prayer rather than on conspiracy theories. "I'll be honest. It's not been easy dealing with this."

A lump forming in the back of my throat dissipates when Taila throws her arms around my neck and gives me a warm hug. "Oh hon, I'm with you all the way."

"Thanks," I say, wiping a gloved hand over the wetness on my cheeks.

"Have you submitted your uni applications yet?" Taila changes the subject while unlocking her scooter.

"Yeah. I managed to get mine in a week before the deadline. How about you?"

"Almost!" she exclaims. "I've got to finish off my personal statement tonight. I'm hoping we both get a place at Imperial College," she says, giving my hand a gentle squeeze.

"Me too."

London is far less expensive than it used to be. Following the wealthy's relocation to rural areas in the wake of the first Covid pandemic, and with efforts put towards improving northern economies through so-called 'levelling up' policies, living costs in England have become more balanced. As far as I'm concerned, Imperial College is the best place to study Politics and Taila really wants to do their Sports Science degree.

Naomi hasn't mentioned her worries about me not getting into uni again, but I can see the way she looks at me, like a shadow has been cast over her hopes. She seems more worried than I am.

I'm currently three-quarters of the way through a classic book – recommended as a cross curricula read for my political studies and literature course – called *Wild Swans* by Jung Chang. It's an autobiography that spans the lives of three generations of women and it's an unputdownable story of power, truth and politics in a Chinese context.

I've just finished reading a section where Chang has written a poem expressing the death of her indoctrinated past and her bewilderment at blundering around in a new world of uncertainties. When a group of 'indoctrination police' called Mrs Shau's Rebels bang on the door of her family home, Chang is terrified of what they will do to her if they find her poem, and she tears it into tiny pieces and throws it in the toilet.

In one sense the story has no similarity to my own as the culture and circumstances are so different, but I am gripped by a sense of the parallels between Chang's world of the Cultural Revolution in the late 1960s and our own contemporary world where truth and meaning can be twisted at the drop of the hat. This idea comes up in our class, but it's always from the point of view of world leaders such as Donald Trump and more recently, President Ming Qang, who would shout 'fake news' as a way of denying truths they didn't want to face. It's unpalatable to refer to Jesus followers as victims of truth-twisting since apparently we've been purveyors of 'oppression' for far too long.

I'm deep in thought when my phone rings. My friend Abdi is calling in holographic mode. I allow him to 'enter'. His lanky shape materialises into cross-legged form on the floor of my room. His image is crystal clear. You can reach out a hand and 'touch' the projected image so that it wavers at the disturbance of light, but still remains. I can imagine how strange and otherworldly this would be to someone of even forty years ago.

"You're such a skank, Sathya," he says, shaking his head and looking around my messy room. To be fair – my room is tidier than usual. There's only one pile of clothes discarded on my bedroom floor and that's literally because I threw them off after entering from school earlier. A few pieces of screwed-up tissue paper are lying near my recycling basket – my aim is not always as accurate as it could be... except when it comes to things that really matter.

"Watch it!" I say, my voice high with irritation. "I didn't have to let you in."

"Why did you, then?" Abdi lets a grin slide over his face.

We've always had this kind of friendship where we both say exactly what we mean in a highly irreverent way. It's fun and I know where I am with him. "Because we're mates," I say.

"Hey," he says, pausing languidly, so that I know this is not just a casual call. "I've been wondering if you're ok, you know, since all this Section 44 stuff? I've noticed you've not been on social media for a while, and that's so not like you."

"Tell me about it," I say, weighing up how much I can tell him. "I've been banned for expressing some Christian beliefs. Maybe I expressed them in a very uncompromising sort of way, but still – that's my right to freedom of speech, surely?" I continue, figuring I can tell him just about as much of that as I want to. Since he's a Muslim and I'm a Christian, I doubt anyone is listening in to our chat right now. 'They' – whoever they are – would be watching out for conversations among my like-believing friends.

"Sheesh, man," he says. "I'm sorry to hear that. Can't believe us Muslims haven't also been targeted for some of the things the fundamentalist types say."

"Maybe we're an easier target now, who knows? But who's to say some of you guys haven't also been targeted?"

"Not that I know of, but we're still in the early days of all this, innit?" Abdi purses his lips in that thoughtful way he has. "I can imagine Muslims getting flack too. The misguided types who think that terrorism is the answer could be the main target, or perhaps not. You've not been banned for that sort of thinking so it could come at us in a completely different way. Blows your mind thinking about it!"

"Absolutely. Thanks for reaching out to check I'm ok, Abdi. I really appreciate it."

"All good, all good, man."

"I'm not a man, in case you hadn't noticed," I josh him.

He reddens. "I know, I know, m..." He stops himself and we both start laughing.

"Hey," I say, giving him a fist bump in the air, "Did you watch the match between Arsenal and Sheffield Wednesday last night?"

I know I've talked about the positives of not being on social media, but the truth is that the difficulties of not being on grate at your sense of self. The most frustrating thing is I can't keep up with some of the discussions and disagreements going on in my friendship groups. I think this is at the heart of what happens next. I feel excluded, like I'm standing on the outside of a tightly knit circle where everyone has their backs to you, and you keep bouncing up to see over their shoulders, but you're too short and the wall of bodies is impenetrable. It's nobody's fault – it's just the way things are.

I try to get to sleep early tonight – early for me is 10pm – but conversations and snippets of things I've read or watched during the day keep playing through my mind. After 45 minutes of tossing and turning, I become aware of the pressure of my bladder. Bad idea having that sneaky caramel latte at 9 o'clock.

Heading past Naomi's room to get to the toilet, I can hear talking from inside. As usual, Naomi has left her door ajar, not wide open, but just enough to hear snippets of conversation. She must be having a holographic meeting as there's more than one person's voice in the room.

"So, T-Team, let's go around the room and share one way in

which we've been thoughtful police of tolerance recently." The speaker is male, whose sound I don't recognise. Believe me, I am not the sort of person who listens in at doors – under normal circumstances – but as soon as I hear the word 'tolerance' my heart gallops, and I stand stock still, holding my breath. I am as close to the door as I can get without my shadow being seen.

Another voice, a female one, says, "I confronted a woman in the street who was swearing at a person of colour for no reason. She was a bit shocked at me confronting her, but she took it really well and stopped her abuse." The voice sounds like she's a young child of no more than ten or eleven, but surely she can't be.

I can hear the murmur of appreciation around the room and for a moment I am caught up in the sense of righteousness, too. "Well done, Sally," the leader says, "You see. It's not as hard as you all might think. Naomi?"

Naomi clears her throat. "I sent a warning to the AI hate trackers to get someone banned for sharing hate speech on social media. She can no longer get on, so isn't a danger to society anymore."

There is another murmur of appreciation, but I am no longer listening. It's like I'm inside a narrow tunnel with a tornado howling around me, and I tiptoe away to the toilet, remembering not to flush as that would alert Naomi that I had been nearby seconds before. (Thankfully, we don't have creaky floors in the hallway as we replaced the original 160-year-old floorboards around five years ago).

As soon as I'm back in my room, I open the window wide and let in a blast of cold air – a shower of senses to counteract my implosion of emotions. That can't be the Naomi I know, can it? But it is. Is there any chance she was talking about someone else? Of course not. The fact she didn't mention my name is evidence of her guilt, her unwillingness to mention the name of the sister she's betrayed. Betrayal – yes, that's what it is! She can use the word 'hate' all she likes to describe my commitment to my faith, but she can't cover up her hateful act.

Every part of me screams out to rush into that room, to stop the meeting and cause a scandal right now, but the small inner voice within me tells me to wait.

I close the window again and shut out the cold air, taking deep, agonising breaths. The pain of my twin's betrayal is a physical stabbing and swelling in my chest. For a moment, I'm worried that I'm having a heart attack or something. But reason tells me this can't possibly be true. Over the roaring in my ears and the pain in my chest, I hear a voice like lapping waves: "Be still and know that I am Lord."

Throwing myself down on my bed, I turn my head into my pillow and allow tears of anger and grief to wrack me. Worn out, I sit up, put on my Dwell Bible app, and listen to the soothing sounds of Felix reading me verse after verse of encouraging words about God's presence in me. His perfect will for my life. His good plans. His own suffering and betrayal.

It's nearly 2am before I feel both peaceful and shattered enough to switch off the light, snuggle under my duvet and delve into a deep sleep.

Chapter 4

As I emerge from sleep to the rousing sound of my 7am alarm, I remember last night's revelation and a hollow, crushed feeling crawls out of my belly. Of course, I've had nowhere near enough rest, adding to my general sense of malaise.

It's Wednesday, so this is a virtual school day, meaning I have plenty of space to confront Naomi. Not that I particularly want to be around her today, but at least I can have things out with her in private. I need to be very careful how I approach this. What I don't want is to be backhanded and snide, no matter how justified I feel.

Emotionally fragile and slightly shaky, I walk down the stairs skirting our dusting bot as it slowly climbs and cleans. It tells me, "Have a nice day, Sathya," in its cheerful voice. Its artificial cheerfulness stings like a rebuke. Mum is passing out of the kitchen into the hallway. She picks up the post scattered on the doormat, spots me and looks up with a warm smile. I need that. I step down into her arms and hold onto her with a lingering embrace, inhaling her distinctive smell of coconut oil and love.

"Sweetpea, is everything ok?" Mum peels herself back from my hug to peruse me.

"Yes, why wouldn't it be?"

"I know my daughter, that's why," she says, her voice deepening.

"Of course you do," I say, keeping my tone light. "Well, yes and no. It's hard to explain, really." To keep her from searching me with those all-seeing maternal eyes, I'll have to give her something. "It's teenage stuff, you know." It's not that I want to hide things from her, but I need to be very careful how I play this, given this is between Naomi and me. It wouldn't be fair to tell Mum what's happened before I've had the chance to talk to Naomi.

"Oh, teenage problems. I remember those too well," Mum says, giving me a sideways squeeze and steering me into the kitchen. "You think I'm too old to remember all the secret yearnings and hormones, but it's all there still stored away inside." She holds a fist against her heart.

"Believe me, it's nothing to do with hormones!" I roll my eyes, secretly enjoying the intrigue and the fact that she's so far off the mark.

As we enter the kitchen, Naomi's slender figure is visible on a Pilates mat near the French windows. We have an open plan arrangement with the kitchen and 'gym' in the same room. Naomi's upper back balances on the ground, and her legs are up in the air, moving backwards and forwards in alternate directions with an elegant scissor-like motion. She does her Pilates exercises for fifteen minutes a day, without fail. She's always been so disciplined.

While Mum begins chopping and frying some onions to make an Indian-style omelette, I cross the floor to where Naomi is lying on the mat, crouch down near her and murmur to her. "Can we talk, immediately after breakfast, please?"

Continuing with her scissor moves, Naomi acts like she's not heard me. For a moment, I visualise myself shoving Naomi and her toppling sideways like a skittle. I take a deep breath to suppress the rebellious image. It might seem like a satisfying thing to do, but it's also glaringly obvious it won't solve the problem for either of us. I do have some self-control. "I know you heard me," I hiss.

Naomi rolls over and sits up. "Of course we can talk, Sathya. Is there any reason we can't simply talk here?"

Now I really want to smack her. My head is tightening like it's being squeezed by a pneumatic exercise band. For a moment, I'm tempted to do exactly what she says and blurt it all out right here with Mum within listening shot, but wisdom holds me back. My heart pounding in my throat, I say, "We *could*, but I would prefer in private."

"Fine," she says heavily.

For goodness' sake! Anyone would think she were being asked to sell her soul rather than simply talk to her sister.

"See you in the attic room at 8:30." That's just fifteen minutes before our first lesson of the day, but hopefully it should be enough time to say what I want to say.

"What are you girls murmuring about in your corner?" Mum calls out over the sound of the frying and the hum of the extractor fan. "Something juicy and interesting I trust!"

"Not really, Mum. You need to get out more," I say, shaking my head.

"No omelette for me, please, Mum," says Naomi, padding like a panther into the kitchen space. "I'll stick with granola and yogurt."

"Omelette is also healthy, you know – egg is a superfood."

"Yeah, but not with the amount of fat that you use. Sorry

Mum, no offence."

Mum sighs. "I'm not a fool, Naomi. It is healthy fat, you know." Naomi's face is unyielding. She will not argue with our resident doctor about healthy and unhealthy fats, but neither will she budge.

"Suit yourself." Mum is clearly disappointed. Feeding us is one of her love languages. "You'll be eating some, won't you, Sathya?"

"Oh yes, wouldn't miss your omelette for the world!" I move close to give Mum a big squeeze.

The air is warm and close in the attic. Nobody sleeps up here unless we have guests, and the room is cosy and tastefully decorated – with cream coloured wallpaper splattered with huge purple flowers and a king-size bed overlaid with a mauve throw. I move over to the skylight to wait for Naomi. The window looks out over the back of our house. Sweeping away below us, the hill drops steeply to the west, with sheep (from here, they look like blobs of beige wool) scattered over the distant fields.

The steep stairs sigh as Naomi comes up behind me. We didn't replace the attic stairs during the renovation, and I'm pleased because we were able to keep some of the older, traditional features of the house. I love history and have seriously considered taking a history degree, but I sense God leading more down the politics route.

Holding a bamboo flask of coffee in her hands, Naomi glances at me as she comes up the stairs and plonks herself down on the edge of the bed. "So, what's this all about then, sweetpea?"

"Don't call me that, please. It's patronising when you use it like that..." I've played this conversation in my mind several times already throughout the night, and I'm determined to get it right. "Don't you feel guilty about what you've done, Naomi?"

Naomi's cheeks flush – perhaps from shame or some other emotion entirely. "What do you know, and how do you know it?" she asks, giving me a direct stare and rubbing the throw between her pinched fingers, just like she used to with her blankie as a small child.

"Last night, I heard you in your room with your T-Team, praising one another for your acts of moral vigilance. I heard you say that you'd banned someone from social media. Of course, you didn't mention my name. But if you don't feel bad about it, I can't think why you didn't say it loud and clear." My throat feels tight and I'm having difficulty swallowing.

"So, you were eavesdropping on me. Hardly a very honourable thing to do." Naomi's eyes are flashing.

"Maybe not," I hiss, "under normal circumstances, but in this case, I'm glad I did. You betrayed me, Naomi! Isn't that far worse than eavesdropping?!"

She stands up and faces me. We're only half a metre apart now. Perhaps she wants to be on the same level as me, I don't know. "Sathya, I did it for your protection, to save you from your dangerous thoughts. I'm sorry if you see it as betrayal. You've got to remember – with the way things are politically – the bots would have picked up..."

I interrupt her. "Dangerous thoughts – what dangerous thoughts?! And if you really wanted to 'save' me, why couldn't you do it in a more upfront way?" I can barely think straight, I'm so angry. I can't believe this is the same girl who I used to share every secret with. The one I laughed and skipped through leaves with. Where is the girl who came to faith with me? The one I trusted with all my deepest desires? In the space of no more than two weeks, she's become someone else. An imposter.

Tears are glistening in Naomi's eyes. "If you continued this path of sharing your faith openly and without discrimination, you'd have been called out eventually, anyway. I don't want to see your life going down the tube, with every opportunity for employment and study closing in on you. And I know Mum and Dad wouldn't want the same for you either!"

"Since when has believing in Jesus been a crime?"

"It's not a crime, but when people feel like you're judging them for not believing what you do, then it's interpreted as a hate crime."

"Oh, my word! So now we can't express what we believe anymore," I say between gritted teeth. "It seems like we've come to a time of persecution again, just like Pastor Daniel was saying the other day. You know, Naomi, that by banning me, you've done just what you said you wanted to avoid – cut me off from my chances of success. Personally, I'm not too worried about it, but you clearly are."

"No!" she blurts. "You were doing it to yourself. You need to learn when to stop and when to keep quiet!"

I say nothing but just look at Naomi, realization drilling down into me.

Arguing with her is not going to change anything. She's following the new status quo. She's become one of them. Her version of tolerance has trampled her faith.

"Hey, class is starting in two minutes," I say calmly, while my inner self swirls in a maelstrom. "We'd better go and get set up." Hopefully, the work will focus my mind, but right now, I doubt I'll be able to focus on my studies today.

Would you, in my situation?

Chapter 5

"**D**o any of you have questions or thoughts regarding what we've learnt so far?" says Mr Baldwick, pausing in his spiel about totalitarianism. My heart is hammering. I always get that when my intuition prods me to say something, but it feels awkward and outside the box to do so.

I raise my screen hand, and Mr Baldwick says, "Yes, Sathya?"

I unmute myself. "Based on what we've learnt so far about the states led by Mao Zedong, Stalin and Hitler, it seems to me that we're moving a little towards totalitarianism in this nation."

"Interesting," he says, raising his thick eyebrows, like he clearly doesn't think so. "Please explain what you mean?"

"Well, at this stage it's quite subtle, but essentially if you have a belief that doesn't fit with the status quo, then you can be cut off from society and lose your rights."

"Does anyone else have an opinion on this?" throws out Mr Baldwick. He doesn't want to grapple with the issue himself, that much is obvious.

Tomasz, an anaemic-looking boy who I don't know well, pipes up to offer his thoughts. "I don't think you're right,

Sathya. In this nation, we have an effective and impartial rule of law and legal system, which protects the vulnerable."

As I listen to him speak, his voice strikes a chord in my memory. This is the same young man who was leading Naomi's T-Team. There's even a slight Eastern European twang to his accent, which I hadn't noticed previously but glares at me now. Tomasz is one of those boys who just blurs into the background, and it sounds mean, but I hadn't registered him being of interest before. Both mesmerised and horrified, I watch his prominent Adam's apple bob up and down yet feel compelled to continue.

"What about Section 44 though? Doesn't that override principles of impartiality?"

Mr Baldwick is monitoring the time, and he curtails the conversation: "This is a very interesting and important discussion, but we need to move on now to exploring Pol Pot and Cambodia. There are less than twelve weeks till our exams, and we have lots to cover still."

I sit back in my seat, gripped by a gnawing frustration. If the conversation is so important, he could have allowed an extra five minutes for further discussion. It would hardly impact on our learning. Baldie's scared of the way the conversation is going and doesn't want me to reveal some hard truths. And the question is – if he's so scared, then why?

It's charcoal black outside. Feathery shadows brush by on either side as I run up the heavily treelined street. Sporadic streetlights cast a dim red glow (red is eco-friendly) from a good height. Since I was fifteen, I've enjoyed my regular evening jogs around the local area. Sometimes, I'll go further afield and manage a three-mile circular run, but most of the time, I run for a short sharp twenty minutes and come straight back. Dad's got used to me running in the dark in the winter time, as I've been doing it for two years now and had no problems, and of course I avoid the parks and other lamp free zones at this time of year. If it was the only exercise I got, I'd probably do more running, but given that running is a mere add-on to my other sporting activities, I'm pretty satisfied with my fitness level. I hope I can maintain it well into my adult life.

My limbs tingling at the intensity of motion, I step just inside the door to the front porch and bounce on the soles of my feet, allowing my breathing to slow down. A triangle of light spills out into the hallway as Dad opens the kitchen door. The hallway light comes on automatically. I take off my trainers and step through the inner glass doorway of the porch to meet him.

"Ah, it's you, sweetpea. I forgot you went out for your run and was wondering what that sound was."

"I do it most days. It's a bit strange of you to forget..."

Dad gets a distant look in his eyes. "You're right. Of course it is. I'm distracted, that's all." He alters his tone to a noticeably perkier one. "Anyway, hope you've managed to work up an appetite. We're having shepherd's pie."

My mouth fills with saliva at the thought. Dad's shepherd's pies are legendary – in our house, at any rate.

Mum's working a late shift, so today is Dad's cooking day. She does, however, do the lion's share of the cooking, simply because she loves it so much. Despite being a senior consultant in oncology, she has wangled a wonderful job share arrangement with a colleague of hers who has recently had a baby. She says it doesn't make much difference to her pay (she gets a decent salary anyway!) and prefers having a good work-life balance.

The kitchen is filled with the aroma of crispy cheese and potato topping and the richness of the meat filling. Dad always uses such an incredible mix of flavours in his fillings that no one else's shepherd's pies quite live up to expectation. Naomi is sitting at the table, her head lowered as she goes through some homework on her tablet. Right now, it's hard for me to see her without snake like thoughts slithering through my mind. I have to make a conscious effort to think positively about her. I remind myself that she is still my sister. She's made in the image of God.

The casserole dish sits in the centre of the table covered by a textile heat preserver, much like an old-fashioned tea cosy. Often, it's the simplest methods that are the most effective and eco-friendly; increasingly as a society, we're returning to simpler, cleaner methodologies. As Dad and I join Naomi, Dad lifts off the heat preserver and steam swirls into the air and quickly evaporates.

We're all unusually quiet until the meal is served out on the plates. At that point, Dad clears his throat and addresses me, "Sathya." There is too much weight in that one word and my heart flip flops. For a start, he's not called me sweetpea, and that means this is serious.

"Yes?" I say, lifting my voice into a question.

"Naomi has been talking to me. She's worried about you..."

I feel a protest rising to my mouth, but quickly stifle it. Let him speak first. I just give a neutral murmur of assent. Naomi glances up at me, then lowers her head again to her plate pretending intense interest in her food.

From across the table, Dad leans forward, places his hand on mine and strokes me with his thumb. He's doing his best here to soften the blow and is struggling with how to raise the topic.

I can't blame him.

"Look here. Maybe now is the time to ease up on your strong Christian stance. You don't have to change what you believe – that would be the opposite of tolerance. But..." and here he draws out the 'u' in that way he has, "it might be best to stop being so vocal about Jesus being the only way. You don't want to lose your chance at getting a good place at university, do you, hmmm?"

My heart is pounding in my ears. I shake my head. "Has Naomi told you what she actually did to me?" My voice comes out high pitched and squeaky.

"I told you – I did it to protect you. You don't want to believe me, but it's true." Naomi gazes at me searchingly. She's positioning herself as the righteous one here. I'm the sinner, the foolish one.

The pounding has turned to a roar. This is not letting up. It's getting worse.

Dad chews slowly on a mouthful of food, buying time. "I know that you girls have your differences, and I don't want to take sides, but I have to say, sweetpea, that I completely agree with nimbycheeks this time. Times have changed and you don't want to be misconstrued as being hateful and judgemental... even if that is not your intention."

I look down at my shepherd's pie and suddenly my food doesn't seem so appetising as it did at first. The roaring between my ears has reached a crescendo. Never mind being like sheep to the slaughter. I'm not ready to roll over panting, presenting my belly for scratching just yet. Unable to hold back the flow anymore, I open my mouth in defence:

"I can't do this. It would be a denial of everything I know to be true. I can understand keeping quiet when I need to keep quiet, but that's not the same as what you're asking me to do. You're asking me to hold back from speaking when I feel I should be speaking, because someone out there will interpret my words as being hate filled. I know what's inside me and it's not hatred. It's love! I could easily become hate filled if this continues, though I will pray every day for that not to happen. Please, just let me be who I am! Can't you see? This is no longer a tolerant society – it's the opposite! If I can't even use social media because you're trying to 'protect me from myself', then everyone should be banned from using it. We're all potentially a danger to ourselves and to others."

I stand up and shove my chair in with more violence than intended. "Sorry Dad, but I'm struggling to be around you both right now. I just need some space."

"Ok, sweetpea. I'll pack up your plate and you can eat it later," says Dad gently. He wants to smother me with kindness, without realising that the kindest thing would be to support me.

"You eat it," I say brusquely. Hot tears fill my eyes, and I head up to my room, barely able to see in front of me. Maybe I should just give up the fight... Maybe none of this is worth it... Maybe I'm just a crazy, blind fool after all...

I turn on my Seeker album on Spotify and allow the faith filled lyrics to swell over me to counteract the barrage of negative thoughts. "You will never fail me, you are my rock and saviour." Then I rummage through the scattered pile of books on my shelf to find my print Bible. I need a physical copy to hold on to, something to devour with my eyes. I flick through the pages of the Bible until I find the passage I want in the book of 2 Corinthians. I read Paul's empowering words and allow them to be my bread, water and healing balm.

"But we have this treasure in jars of clay to show that this all-surpassing power is from God and not from us. We are hard pressed on every side, but not crushed; perplexed, but not in despair; persecuted, but not abandoned; struck down, but not destroyed. We always carry around in our body the death of Jesus, so that the life of Jesus may also be revealed in our body."

The nail-biting reality of suffering is there, yet all imbued with light and a hollering, drum-pounding, feet-stamping perseverance. A few more verses down and I soak up the following – "For our light and momentary troubles are achieving for us an eternal glory that far outweighs them all. So we fix our eyes not on what is seen, but on what is unseen, since what is seen is temporary, but what is unseen is eternal."

There's a lump in my throat when I finish reading the chapter, discerning that there's more pain to come. Yet warmth surges through me. A settled spirit. A determined mind.

Chapter 6

"Sathya," breathes Taila down the phone. "You're first on my list of people to call. Dad told me that things are heating up, and it's going to be best for us to stop having holographic, online meetings for a while. The security risk is too high."

Mayeso, Taila's dad, has a close relationship with Pastor Daniel and is part of the church leadership team. So Mayeso frequently finds things out earlier than the rest of us.

"Why doesn't that surprise me?" I am hunched over painting my toenails a navy blue flecked with silver, but the awkwardness of my position can't stop my cynicism bursting through. "Don't tell me – the state spies are keeping tabs on the online meetings of all Christian gatherings now."

"Pretty much," says Taila. "Apparently, we're going to try meeting in different families' homes, not always the same place, to make sure that 'they' can't easily track us down. But this first week, we're meeting in the city centre at Cafferty's on the Moor."

"Really?" I blow gently on my little toe, and it dries immediately. "Seems a bit public." Cafferty's is a trendy bar that opened around five years ago.

"We'll be using the function room in their basement. One of their staff is also a follower of Jesus and has helped out with this temporary arrangement."

"That's good to know. I have to say part of me is excited by this new move," I say. "The very fact that we might get caught!"

Taila chuckles. "Good to see you've not lost your sense of adventure." She pauses and I can hear her noisy breathing – sounds like she's got a cold or something. "I know that things haven't been easy for you recently. How are things between you and Naomi?"

"The same," I say, shrugging my shoulders. "She's not budged in her thinking one bit, and Mum and Dad are pretty much on the same page as her. I'm just getting on with it, to be honest. It's a lonely place at home. Superficially, things are normal, but I can't share anything meaningful with them right now. It would feel too false."

"That must be so hard," Taila says. "The closest I've had to that is that Regina is no longer talking to me. I must have said something to offend her, though I can't think what... But thankfully it hasn't gone wider than that unlike with you. Oh, and one other thing: we're not going to be having whole church gatherings now, we're just going to stick with smaller groups meeting in a variety of different locations. Instead of having our usual youth meeting, we'll be meeting in all-age small groups so that we don't lose the full flavour of being church together."

"Are we going to be in the same group?" I say, leaning back on my bed and flexing out my bare legs to see my toes in their fully polished glory. I don't want to be too clingy, but it would make things harder than they already are not having her there.

"Yeah, we are. Pastor Daniel is aware of what you're going

through and knows you need friends around you. I'll see you on Wednesday then? Shall we meet at the top of the Moor near where the bike stands are at 7:20pm? We can then walk down together."

It's a cloudless January evening – one of those evenings where it's so cold you can see your breath in the air and early frost glistens on the pavement. I've just locked up my scooter and stand with my chilly hands stuffed into my jacket pockets, waiting for Taila. Trust me to forget my gloves on a night like tonight. Given that Christmas has passed, you don't expect the streets to be filled with pedestrians. But things are different tonight.

I hear the chanting before I see the cause and turn towards the sound. A crowd of people – mostly young – are pouring en masse down the road from the Peace Gardens. They're all dressed up warm for winter with puffer jackets, gloves and woollies galore. They spill across the road towards me in a jostling, marching force, calling out repeatedly, "T for tolerance, T for tolerance! Keep up the vigilance, keep up the vigilance!" Some of them are holding up banners, some of them are gesturing aggressively. As the crowd flows past me, two teenagers – one boy and one girl (no older than fourteen) look at me then each other, and separate on either side of me, signalling in my direction. They hold up their right hands in a straight line and prod down their stiff left hands onto the fingers of their right, forming a t. The girl's heart-shaped face scrunches up into a fierce moue of contempt, which is especially shocking to me, as she would seem so sweet otherwise. On my right, the boy's forceful action reminds me of a much ruder gesture. The boy and girl glance backwards as they pass me, merge and link arms as they continue with their march.

I freeze. That certainly felt personal and intentional. For a second, I wonder if their aggression was a racial thing targeted at my olive skin, but I quickly dismiss it. The boy was unmistakeably Middle Eastern.

I couldn't possibly count, but at an estimate there must be five-hundred or so in the crowd, and they flow down the Moor towards the council offices at the far end, most of them passing well by me. I think I spot Tomasz in the crowd but can't be sure. I certainly hope Naomi is not among them, but it's impossible to tell. As the last dregs of the crowd pass, I spot Taila scootering towards me, unsmiling.

"Are you ok?" she asks, pulling up her scooter and securing it to a stand. "Looks like you got caught up right in the crowd."

"Yeah, I'm fine. It's a bit unsettling though, don't you think? Did you hear what they were chanting?"

Grim faced, she nods. I tell her about the teenage couple, and she snorts. "It's like the Hitler Youth. I'm gobsmacked as to why No one can see it."

"Tell me about it. Nobody wants to see it. It's such a perversion of what they say they believe."

We link arms to stroll down the brightly lit pedestrianised walkway towards Cafferty's. I keep my hands stuffed in my pockets.

Cafferty's shop window evidences a softly lit interior, with a smattering of customers, most of whom are well away from the window. Our entrance way is on the left-hand side. We speak into the old-fashioned intercom system and when we hear "Hello" through the crackle, Taila mouths out each letter carefully, "KCC". It's the code word we've been told to use, so that whoever is answering the door knows to let us through. It stands for Kairos Community Church.

"Come down, please."

The door swings open and we go down a flight of threadbare carpeted steps to the basement.

"Welcome, welcome!" As we pass through swinging doors into the steamy heat of the function room, I'm clamped in a whiskery bearhug. Grinning delightedly under the embrace, I look over his shoulder at Taila being embraced by Marie, Angus's petite redheaded wife. Angus and Marie release us and swap over. Marie gives a jolly "oooh," sound as she hugs me. Afterwards, we all look at one another and laugh. Angus and Marie are in their early fifties and are part of the church leadership team. Personally, I don't know them very well, since I've spent most of my time in the youth group, but they radiate warmth wherever they go. "So, we'll be looking after you two for the unforeseen future alongside your wonderful dad," Angus nods at Taila. "I hope yous can cope with us both!" Angus says, giving a belly laugh.

"Of course!" I say, glancing at Taila and grinning again. I had been feeling a bit nervous about not being part of my usual peer group, but all that has melted away. The small, low-ceilinged room contains no more than twenty-five people. It's a fraction of the size of our church. Tentatively, I glance around. The room contains a wide variety of people from a toddler scrambling around on the chairs through to our resident long-term asylum seeker, Abdul. In the mix, I spot two other teenagers – siblings Marlene and Dan. Their presence makes me aware of Naomi's absence like a missing tooth. We walk over, say hi and sit down, drinking squash and waiting for the meeting to start.

Angus walks into the centre of the room with his pint glass and plonks it down on a table. The hubbub of noise around the room quietens until the only sound is two-year-old Darius humming tunelessly to himself. He looks at Marie, and says good-humouredly, "Seems I don't need to call on your help to get this lot's attention then."

Arms folded, Marie shrugs. "I could do it for you anyway, if you like," and she opens her mouth, and expands her chest as if she's about to make an announcement, then does a theatrical about turn and closes her mouth tightly.

Of course, everyone laughs. Eight-year-old Aaron, who is Taila's brother, laughs the loudest. It's one thing that drew me to this church at the very beginning. The way that they were so fun and down to earth alongside their unmistakable, committed passion for Jesus.

"It's great fun meeting with you all in this way," Angus says, taking a sip from his beer and beginning proceedings, "But of course we're not meeting this way for the heck of it. We're meeting like this because of that pesky new legislation that you will've heard about – Section 44. For those of you who've been living with your head in the sand for the past few months – yes you, Mayeso" – Angus winks at Taila's dad – "that essentially means that if we say something that could be seen as 'offensive' by anyone else then we could have our freedoms curtailed. As Christians who believe in the power of the cross, which Paul says is 'an offence to those perishing' it seems like we're really at the losing end of this legislation. Sadly, it's no longer safe to gather like we have been doing, as it is possible that we're being watched." He looks around the room at everyone quietly listening.

"I'm sorry, but I don't believe in pretending that bad things are not happening for the sake of protecting children, and I'm sure that you parents will be able to explain all this to your kids in a way they can understand. One thing we can be sure of is that we're living in a time of persecution not seen by Christians in the West during our lifetime. Let's all be vigilant as to what's really going on here, and remember that persecution can strengthen our faith rather than diminish it. That's me done for now. Before Daniel takes the mic for the Word, I'll pass you onto Marie, who's leading us in a time of worship."

Worship is a mixture of singing songs and other creative activities. At one point, Marie gets us all down on the floor with sheets of paper and a stash of paints, pens, pencils and various craft materials. While she strums on her guitar in the background, we all form shapes, images and words that reflect the concept of God as creator. Finding myself in a peaceful flow, by the end of the ten minutes that Marie gives to the task, I have painted a swirl of glorious colours in the middle of my page and stuck some biodegradable glitter around the edge of the swirls. Satisfied, I sit back in my chair with my knees pulled up to my chest. At that moment, something happens in my inner being, which is hard to describe. An inexplicable joy fills me. It's like I'm being strengthened in my core. I may not be capable by myself, but with God's spirit in me, I can stand firm against all the twisty, sneaky lies.

"Are you ok?" Taila whispers to me.

"Yeah, why wouldn't I be?" It's only then that I realise my cheeks are damp, and I give Taila a tearful smile. Taila gives my shoulders a squeeze. She knows exactly what I'm going through.

Chapter 7

You need to understand a few things have taken place in the past few years in the UK, laying the foundations for where we're at now. One is that the distinction between left and right in politics has blurred. It started back in the 2020 Covid pandemic when a newly formed Conservative government established one of the hugest state funded schemes of all time – the furlough scheme, where essentially thousands of workers had their salaries paid for them by the state to prevent the rising cases. Now, we are governed by a populist party called The Unity Party. David Zinder, one of generation Z, is the youngest British Prime Minister for a few hundred years. He's only 41. The whole point of a populist party is that they represent the will of the people, which, as you can imagine, sounds good – but in practice doesn't always work, as what they stand for is constantly shifting.

Secondly, in the last two decades genuine followers of Jesus have become an even smaller minority and no longer have the backing of the so-called established church. Without a leader who possesses both spiritual and political authority (like the Archbishops of Canterbury used to), we have lost ground when it comes to our rights being respected. Despite claiming to protect minorities from oppression, those who advocate the tolerance agenda exclude Christians from the minority category. Being a politics geek, I've been reading, watching and thinking a lot about this, and a few weeks ago, Daniel did a study on this topic in our church meeting.

So, where are we now? Saturday 1st February 2041. The shower door shuts with a hollow clang as I step out, to be greeted by a high-pitched whooping sound emerging from Naomi's room. Let me guess – she's not hurt herself, she's excited by something. I don't have long to find out. I wrap a towel turban style around my hair and put on my bathrobe.

Just as I leave the bathroom, Naomi powers out of her room, jumping and cavorting like Mulan on speed. To be honest, you rarely see her like this. I stifle a laugh. Seeming to forget all our differences, she spots me and squeals, "I got a place at Oxford!"

I give her a hug, and say, "That's great, nimbycheeks!"

"Do you think Mum and Dad heard?" she asks, before twisting her lips to one side.

"Er, probably. I'm not sure..."

As if in answer to her question, Mum pops her head out of their bedroom door on the other side of the corridor. "Did we hear what?"

I laugh. "Naomi's got into..." I nod at Naomi, giving her the right to tell.

"Oxford!!!" she squeals again.

As Mum and Dad both emerge and celebrate with Naomi, I slip away down the stairs. I am pleased for her, I really am. But I am also aware of a forlorn ache in the pit of my stomach; so far, I've heard nothing from any of my university choices. Naomi's probably right. I...

No. It's best for me not to think about it or make any

assumptions until I have a definite response. If I've heard nothing by the end of the month, I can chase them up.

The winter sun splashes brightness against the glass walls of the nearby shop fronts, reminding me how much I've got to be grateful for. I love the sun. In that sense, I would have been happier being raised in India. Sometimes I imagine what it would have been like if Mum and Dad had lived there rather than here. After all, they met in India during the Covid years, though that's another story... I'm standing next to one of the cylindrical metallic fountains in St Paul's square between the graceful arc of the Winter Gardens and the Peace Gardens, watching the silvery water flowing endlessly over the fountain. It's mesmerising. After a few minutes, Abdi's lanky dark figure appears, late as usual. He gives me a lopsided, apologetic grin.

"Sorry, I'm late. I got caught up helping my dad with fixing something."

"Yeah, yeah, always an excuse," I say, and give him a friendly elbow nudge.

Abdi's so laid back that we would stand bantering in the cold for ages if it were down to him. So, I take the next move and flick forward a few pages. "Let's go to Santi's for a latte then." Santi's is a new trendy café in the city centre, beloved by teens and twenty-somethings. The fact that it's not a chain but manages to maintain quality and value is a huge part of its appeal.

"Great," Abdi says, "You lead."

A few minutes later, we're sitting on opposite sides of the table in a window booth, slouched in huge, colourful cushions on the otherwise functional wooden furniture. A waiter hands both of us tall, wide topped caramel lattes sprinkled with cinnamon.

"Anyone would think we're on a date or something," Abdi says, waiting for me to start drinking before he starts his. I know he's being polite, but it annoys me somehow. I don't want him deferring to me all the time. It makes me uncomfortable.

"Why? Because we're drinking the same drink? Hardly," I say. Abdi and I have been friends since we started high school. I can't even begin to imagine him in a romantic way.

He chuckles. I squint at the rectangle of fuzzy hair on his chin, then away again. This is awkward. "Can we change the subject, please?" I request, squirming.

"It's not that bad..."

"Zip it," I interrupt, drawing an imaginary line across my lips. I want him to be clear I mean it, but in a playful enough manner to not offend him.

Shaking his head, he lowers his eyes to his glass, acting like he's deeply interested in his latte all of a sudden. "Have you heard anything back from your uni applications?"

"Not yet. But Naomi found out this morning that she got into her top choice so she's over the moon." I elongate the 'oo' sound for effect.

"It's just a matter of time before you'll hear back," he says, casually, "And you'll get the place of your dreams, inshallah."

"I'm not so sure," I say. "But we'll see. Have you decided what you want to do next year?"

He licks one finger, then uses it to circle the rim of his glass, gradually building up speed and friction. A high-pitched ringing rises. I try to do the same, but nothing happens. "Press down firmer," he instructs.

Still no sound. "I give up," I say. "Not with life in general," I say, "Just this!" We laugh. "Anyway, you've not answered my question yet."

"You know what Somali parents are like. They really want me to go to uni, but I can't face them spending all that money on me when all I want is to set up my own restaurant chain. I can picture it already. A whole mix of Somali and other East African foods with a fun, welcoming vibe, a bit like the Mexican food chain – Chiquitos."

"Sounds good," I say, cupping my chin in my hand. "Won't it help to get a business management degree or something? And don't you want the whole experience of living away from home?"

Abdi shakes his head. "I don't think so. It's all drunkenness and sleeping around as far as I can tell. I'm thinking of taking smaller practical training courses. Would be much better than getting into debt."

"Well, good on you for knowing what you want to do and sticking to your guns," I say.

At five o'clock, I use my phone and login to my university application tracing app, expecting to see nothing again. It's Saturday after all. But Naomi got a reply today, and there's no blanket rule banning communication on Saturday, especially given there could be delays in the system if it's overloaded.

I stare at the screen. My heart hammers because blue dots are showing on my screen next to all three of my applications. Communication at last. Hovering over each dot, I can get a preview of each communication. My top choice – Imperial College – says 'Outcome: Rejected. Reason: Unsuitable.' Further down next to my second choice – Durham University – I hover and see 'Outcome: Rejected. Reason: Unsuitable.' My body is quivering all over. I don't even want to read the last one.

But there it is. Sheffield University. The same awful wording.

This is brutal. I put down my phone and lower my head into my hands. My mind rattles like falling dominoes through all the possible reasons I could be unsuitable for a place at university. I'm too sporty, I'm mixed race, I'm too slim, I'm too political.... None of them makes any sense. The only plausible reason is the one that Naomi highlighted when all this began: I'm too outspoken in my faith, and I've been banned on social media. Do the universities really go along with this kind of thinking? Clearly they do, otherwise I wouldn't be receiving these inexplicable rejections. All in one go! It's like they were waiting to corroborate each other's intel before they made their decisions. I groan.

There's a gentle rap on my door. "Are you ok in there?"

Mum. No way. Trust her to be in the corridor at the wrong moment. I hadn't realised how loudly I'd groaned. I calculate quickly. There's no point in lying to her, and I don't even want to.

I sigh. "You can come in," I say. It's no good talking to her through a closed door.

Mum enters the room and sits down next to me on the bed. I sense exactly what she's going to say when I tell her. It won't make any difference to what I need to do.

"Look, I say," picking up my phone and showing her the decisions.

"Oh, sweet Sathya," she says, cupping my chin in her hands. "I'm so sorry this had to happen to you." There's an unspoken 'but' hanging in the air.

"Had to?" I ask, watching her face closely, a lump in my throat. She releases my chin.

"Well, yes. It's painful, but it's necessary to get you to

understand you can't keep up with this..."

"With my faith, you mean?" I want my voice to sound firm and determined, but it comes out all in a wobble.

"Not exactly with your faith, but the expression of your faith. We've been through this, Sathya. You know how things are. Look at where Naomi is now. She's made the best choice."

I'm dumbfounded. I want to lash out, defend, and justify, but instead, I feel like I'm crumbling. Maybe they're all right? Maybe, just for the sake of my future, I should toe the line, swat my pesky principles down like a fly?

Then Daniel's most recent preach about Peter's denial of Jesus comes to mind. The cock crowing three times gave Peter a stark reminder of his betrayal. I know that I can't throw away my principles, don't want to do it. It's painful not being able to fulfil my dreams of university, but that's not going to change my determination to stand firm. Jesus came to give his followers life in all its fullness, and I have to trust him in how things work out. He's not some sort of genie providing us with instant wish fulfilment. His plans are bigger than that, more centred around his kingdom purposes.

I could answer Mum with another defensive challenge, but instead I say, "Mum – you know that's hurtful to me," and tears fall past all the barbs in my throat. "But I won't stop loving you, or Naomi or Dad. And I'm NOT giving in."

Mum knows when to keep quiet. She hugs me, then her sari rustles as she gets up and walks out of the room to leave me be.

Chapter 8

Naomi is tramping a few feet ahead of me up the street towards our house. We've not said a word the entire way home from school. My feelings are too raw, like a recently formed blister. If I open my mouth, nothing good will come out, so it's better to say nothing. She glances back at me, and I slow down slightly to maintain the physical distance.

"Oh, grow up," she says, tossing me a glare. "There's no need to be all high and mighty with me. It's not my fault you didn't get into your uni choices. I did warn you!"

My head pulses with rage, and my shoulders stiffen. I want to spit back all my vitriol. But if I do that, the temporary satisfaction I get will only congeal into a sticky mess. Instead, heart pounding, I say, "You did, indeed. Can't I just choose to keep quiet for now? I don't want to make this harder for either of us than it already is."

"Suit yourself," she says sulkily, and continues up the hill.

"Are you still feeling it, hon?" Taila's solid and friendly holographic image plonks down in my room later that evening. I stop swivelling on my office chair. It's a bad habit I've got into. It's a strangely comforting motion.

"Good question," I say. "Yes, is the simple answer. Honestly – in one day to get Naomi's acceptance and all three of my rejections, I'd say deserves some pain on my part. The harsh part is that there's absolutely nothing I can do about it. If I contact the universities and ask them to explain my 'unsuitability', what are they going to say that will make any difference? Whatever they say can't make things better. They can't tell me 'Your predicted grades aren't high enough' cos that simply isn't true. They can't tell me, 'you're a social outcast because you're on the banned list for hateful speech' cos that would be too direct, and that's not how this kind of control works. The state won't tell us all the consequences of people's failure to comply with the tolerance norms, will they? And it's not on the mainstream media, is it? It wouldn't suit their agenda at all."

"Such a dilemma," says Taila, chewing her lip. Moisture glistens in her eyes. She's feeling my pain.

"No, there's no dilemma, just a long, dark tunnel."

"I feel bad cos even though I'm as passionate for God as you are, I've not experienced any personal backlash – yet." Taila twiddles her hair extensions around her fingers, thoughtfully.

If I'm honest, I had a pang of jealousy when I heard that Taila got into Imperial College. She got her result first thing this morning and told me at school. I wanted so much to be pleased for her, but it stung all the same. I clear my throat. "Don't even begin to think like that. This is random. Because I'm now on the blacklist, I'm an easy target."

"Maybe I should be more vocal about my faith. I don't want you to be alone in this."

I'm genuinely touched. "Taila, that's so sweet of you. But please, just support me as you are. I don't need you to be going through persecution. Wouldn't it be selfish of me to want that?"

I laugh wryly.

"Not really. I'd understand," Taila says. She's perfectly serious. She lifts her head and says with a flash in her eyes, "How about you take this further and try to claim discrimination? We could ask Dad to help you. He's got some good legal contacts."

Taila's onto something here. Even if the state is against 'hate crime', surely there must be lawyers who could help us argue that I've not committed hate crime. This could help me get a place at uni after all...

The trouble is I feel like I'm sludging through sinking sand. I'm not sure if I have the fire to push for this right now. The political agenda is weighted against me already. Won't I just be labelled as even more of a 'troublemaker' than I already am?

"I'm not sure, Taila. It sounds good, but I feel unsettled about it somehow. I'll let you know."

A few minutes after Taila's shape disperses from my room, my phone rings again. I'm surprised to see Marie's number. I accept her incoming alert as a standard call and tuck my legs under me in my armchair near the window to which I've moved.

"Hi Sathya, it's Marie from church. How are you doing?" she asks breezily.

For safety reasons, we're currently not meeting on Sundays, so I haven't had the chance to mention my news to anyone from our group other than Taila. There must be a reason why Marie's called that goes beyond mere friendliness. She's never called me before.

"Not great, to be honest. I found out at the weekend that I've been rejected from all three of my uni choices."

"Oh, Sathya, that's awful. I'm so sorry. Did they give any reason why?"

"Not really. I just got 'unsuitable' – whatever that means. I can only assume that it's got something to do with me being banned on social media."

"You're not the only one," Marie says. "I don't know anyone else in our church, but I am aware of a few from other churches. It's the first time I've heard of someone as young as yourself though, I must say. Let's try to see it in a positive light. You must be doing something right! It might seem strange, but it's only those who are communicating truth unashamedly who seem to be on the receiving end of these type of restrictions."

I snort lightly. "I can try and look at it that way, Marie!"

"Oooh," and here Marie sounds like she's comforting a baby, "But it can't be easy, sweetheart."

My legs tingle with an uncomfortable fuzzy feeling and I stretch them out several times to relieve the pins and needles. It's hardly surprising. My position has become awkward and tensed. "It's not," I say, and my voice breaks.

"Actually, Sathya, I'm calling because I was praying for you and a few other church members last night, and I felt God give me a very specific word for you. It's not an easy one though. Are you happy for me to share it with you?"

"Please do," I say. I pick at the seam of my jeans, pulling at the threads. This habit of mine is one of Naomi's pet hates.

"I felt that you should buy a portable GPS. It was something I was thinking about anyway for our members – with the dangers of being tracked on your phone – but the impression that I had of you at this time was so strong that I knew I had to let you know. It makes sense now when you told me what you did. It's like you need to be extra vigilant. The Holy Spirit was giving a clear warning."

A strange thrill runs through me. At first, I can't tell if it's fear or excitement, then I realise that it's a mixture of both.

"Thanks for sharing your impression with me." I'm still a new enough believer that I can't quite get used to the fact that God cares enough about me to speak to me through other people. "I'll certainly bear what you've said in mind."

One of the advantages of online school is flexibility. The next day I sign up for late-learning for my afternoon lessons before heading out at lunchtime to the city centre. The school discourage us from using this too much as they want us to engage with the interactive element of the lessons, but you're allowed up to five late-learning periods each half term.

You have to be 18 before you can buy things online and my and Naomi's birthday is not until June. So, at the moment, I'm taking advantage of Mum and Dad's Bi-pay option, which allows me to purchase using their account on the high street.

One particular shop is on my radar. It's a small indie down one of those lovely commercial alleyways – Chapel Walk – called Gid Gaj. Even when I'm not spending any money, I love browsing in here. There's quirky stuff from all the way back in the 1990s till now from bobble removers (the kind that you roll over knitted items) through to funky thermal socks and everything in between – whether futuristic or new retro. The bespectacled shopkeeper smiles at me when I enter. He knows me as well as you know anyone who frequents a business of yours.

"Can you give me any advice regarding portable GPS please?" I say, swanning up to the counter and removing my gloves.

"Sure," the shopkeeper says, wrinkling his nose to hoist his glasses up. He takes out a range of different GPS of all styles and shapes and lays them out on the counter for me. Then he looks up and attempts to explain the different types to me while

I nod and ask pertinent questions.

"I want something very small and with one track functionality." According to the shopkeeper's explanation, this is perfect for me since it means that I can't be tracked by anyone else.

He pops a compact, black machine into my hand. It's about the size of an old two-pound coin. Small enough to fit in a pocket without being noticeable. "You can have this in blue, black or silver."

"This one's great," I say.

"It'll set you back £45. Are you going to pay by card or Bi-pay?"

"It'll have to be Bi-pay," I say, pleased that I appear mature enough to be given the option.

"And do you want to itemise the bill to your parent's account?"

"No, thanks. The name of the shop is enough." They can't know I'm buying a GPS as they'll get suspicious.

He places the biometric machine in front of me, and I wave my forefinger lightly over the reader. Frowning, he looks down at the machine. "Can you try again please?"

This time, I hold my finger motionless over the reader. The skin prickles on the back of my neck. Something's not right.

"I'm really sorry," he says, shaking his head. "Your account has been blocked."

Chapter 9

I meander along Chapel Walk in the direction of Fargate, staring abstractly ahead. My head is spinning and my throat is tight. *Can't I buy anything anymore? What is wrong with these people? Am I so dangerous I need to be that tightly controlled? I'll have to ask Taila to buy my GPS for me. At least she can – for now, anyway.*

"Oy, watch where you're going!"

I stumble into a stack of bread sticks, crisp packets and wrapped sandwiches piled on the pavement at the man's feet. My heart racing, I right myself, then bend down to the sitting man. "I'm so sorry, totally my fault. Here, let me help you."

"Get lost, I can sort it mysen," the man says, grimacing at me and yanking his hat further forward.

When we became a cashless economy eight years ago, that took away one of the methods of dealing with homeless people – tossing change at them. Of course, homelessness didn't disappear, so instead of cash, passers-by who want to help give small items purchased like takeaway food, drinks, socks and gloves.

Reeling a little from the rebuff, I consider further action, but realise he's not in the right place to receive anything from me now, so I walk slowly away.

I'm just passing out of the alleyway into pedestrianised Fargate, when I spot a young woman wearing a high vis jacket and carrying a tablet heading towards me. Her beaming face has got speak-to-me written all over it. I can't help noticing her purple-streaked brown hair is piled so high on top of her head it would be precarious if there were any risk of it falling. Under normal circumstances, I'd politely sidestep people trying to do market research or sell me things on the streets, but I'm feeling so disgruntled that I'm in the mood for a rant.

"Hey there, I'm wondering if you'd be able to answer a few questions for me on social and political issues? It won't take more than ten minutes of your time."

"Which company are you working for?" I stop walking to engage with her.

"Tarvo," she says, continuing to smile and waving an ID badge at me. "We're an independent think tank – nothing to do with the government, anyway!" She gives me a knowing laugh.

I've vaguely heard of Tarvo. So, why not? I don't have to rush back for my classes as I can take them at any time of day, as long as they're completed before midnight.

"Sure. I can spare a few minutes."

"Thanks, you won't regret it," the woman says, pushing back a strand of hair that has slipped from her elaborate arrangement. "My name is Lisa, by the way," she says, putting out a hand for me to shake. I take her hand. "Shall we go and sit over there on that bench while we go through the questions?"

We sit down on the bench. Lisa sits a metre away from me and runs her finger over her screen, preparing her tablet for the questionnaire.

She starts off by asking a few basic questions – age range, socio economic band of my parents, my religion, their religion, political affiliation. Then she moves onto asking more probing questions. "How much do you know about the new Section 44 legislation: a good deal, a little, not much, or nothing?"

"A good deal," I say.

"How do you feel about the legislation? This is the opportunity for you to give an open response. Nobody's listening apart from me so you can be as honest as you like."

Energy pulses through me. This is my opportunity to get my frustrations out.

"It's discriminatory and oppressive. It claims to protect people against hate crime, but it's hateful towards those who do not follow the status quo. It claims to be in favour of tolerance but it's actually the total opposite."

Lisa has her head lowered on her screen, recording my wording. She looks up at me. "You're not the only one who thinks so," she says, pursing her lips.

"Aren't you supposed to be independent?" I laugh.

"We are," she says tersely. "I'm just conveying the reality of other people's responses, not giving an opinion." Her mouth twitches at the corners.

"You mentioned that you're a Christian, so I've now got a series of questions to ask in relation to your faith. I'm going to read out a list of statements related to Christian faith. I want you to say 'Agree, disagree, or unsure' in relation to each statement."

Caution tugs at my heels, but I kick it down. She's told me this is independent, so it's not going to be filed away in some government department. "Fire away."

"Number 1. Love is at the heart of what it means to be a

Christian."

"Agree," I say.

"Number 2. Charity and doing good works are important to me."

"Agree." This is all harmless so far.

"Number 3. Jesus is the way, the truth and the life."

Watching a pigeon pecking the ground for crumbs, I'm tempted to give a noncommittal response. Then warmth rises in me, and I say, "Agree."

This goes on for a couple more minutes before the questions move to my opinions about government spending and priorities. Several of the questions are open-ended questions giving me the chance to express myself in my own words.

Eventually, Lisa inhales loudly and closes the cover on her screen. "Well, that's all for now. Thank you so much for your time. We really appreciate your honesty and will use your ideas to help develop thinking around these areas." Lisa smiles at me again and stands up to shake my hand. Something hard and abrasive rubs against my fingers. Wondering what it is, I look down. There's a ring on her finger. It's a silver-plated ring with a chunky letter T embossed on it.

A firecracker explodes in my heart. Impossible!

There's nothing to say you can't innocently wear a T-ring on their finger. T for Tony, T for timely, T for any other word in the dictionary beginning with t. Despite telling myself this, I tremble as Lisa parts with me and walks away. I feel as though I've exposed myself in the streets and everyone is staring at me.

During our conversation, slate grey clouds have gathered. A fine drizzle begins, building up pace as I walk home, unable to shake my discomfort.

Chapter 10

"Sorry, I missed your call. I've just come out of English Literature." Taila sounds breathless, as if she's been running.

"It's ok, Taila. Don't panic." I should try listening to my own advice some time. "Just a quick one. If I text you the details, would you be able to buy me a portable GPS please? I can't."

"What do you mean, you can't?"

"It's a long story. It seems that I've been blocked from spending money on top of everything else."

"Oh hon, I'm so sorry." Taila is quiet for a moment, then sighs heavily. "It doesn't seem fair that you should be going through all this while I..." I can picture her swallowing hard to hold back tears. "I will do whatever I can to help you," she says, her warrior spirit shining through. "Send me the details. I've got to go, Dad's calling me. Keep your spirits up."

"Speak soon," I say, letting the phone fall from my hand onto the sofa.

Slumping back into the sofa, I gaze at the oil painting on the wall above the fireplace and am struck by something for the first time. It depicts the story of the tribal boy Ekalavya, who desired to become one of the best archers in the world.

Unfortunately, he has an incredibly hard master, who asks him to cut off his thumb because of the jealousy of another student he values more. Without any questioning, Ekalavya cuts off his thumb and is unable to achieve his goal. In the painting, the boy's thumb is lying in a pool of brilliant red in an otherwise brown and green picture. He's bowing down to his master in submission.

Whenever Mum told us this story when we were kids, she would always say, "Sacrificing in order to achieve our ambitions can lead to pain, but loyalty and respect is most important." She's blind to the parallels in my life. In refusing to be disloyal to my God, I have lost a few appendages on the way. Have I got any more to lose? Is it worth it?

Bing bong bing bong, bing bong bing bong. The doorbell. I've always been slightly embarrassed that it sounds like a grandfather clock, though there's no good reason why. One of those strange kiddie things that's stuck. "I'll get it!" I holler to avoid anyone else in the family rushing down the stairs to open it.

I wave my hand over the door sensor and it edges open into the porch. I'm surprised to see Abdi rubbing his cold hands at the entrance way. (Trust him to forget his gloves!) He doesn't usually turn up like this, without any warning. I like spontaneity so I'm happy, though I'm also painfully aware of the two hours of unfinished study I need to complete this evening.

"What's up?" I greet him. "It's not like you to just rock up out of the blue."

Abdi gives me a lopsided grin and takes off his shoes. "I know. It's bad, isn't it? I won't stay long."

Swishing down the stairs behind us, Mum enters the hallway, pats me playfully on the behind and gushes at him: "Ignore the high and mighty one. You're most welcome! Are you staying for dinner, sweetheart?"

Since when did she start calling my male friends sweetheart? I mouth sweetheart at him sarcastically and he blushes.

"Are you going to stay a little longer?" Mum says, scraping food scraps from our plates into the incinerator.

"You can stay till 7:30, if you like," I say, making eye contact with Abdi across the table. "I've still got to get my afternoon lessons done unfortunately, and I don't want to be studying too late."

"You can join us in the lounge after you two young'uns are done with your chitchat, if you like," Dad offers. "We'll probably be watching a good comedy on the old Goggle box."

"Thanks, sir," he says. "I might take you up on that one."

Dad has given up on trying to correct Abdi for calling him sir, so he doesn't bat an eyelid. Abdi is effortlessly respectful.

"Have a good time, guys," Naomi carols in Abdi's direction, "I'm just going up to get my homework done." Watching the familiar curve of her back as she slips out of the kitchen, cradling her bamboo flask, my head tightens. I can't help noticing that Naomi has avoided talking directly to me all evening. Something is bothering her, whether guilt or something else, I can't be sure. It's hard not being close to her anymore. I miss the D & Ms we used to have. Even if I wanted to, there's already such a glaring gap between us, a shift in our dynamics, which I can't pretend isn't there.

Picking up a small paper packet of chocolate biscuits to snack on, Abdi and I head upstairs. We scoot past my bedroom up to the attic room. In my opinion, there's something a little too intimate about bringing him to my bedroom. It's not the same as a holographic meeting. I don't want him to get the wrong idea.

"I love your parents," Abdi says, curling himself up on a cushion against the wall. "They're always so warm and friendly."

"Yes," I say, sitting down a few feet away from him. "They are. It helps that I'm not living in an icebox, but sometimes, you know, they can kill you with their kindness..."

"What d'ya mean?"

I push the packet of biscuits to him, and he picks one out and turns it over in his fingers.

"It's difficult to explain really, but they're not exactly supporting me in my decision to stick to my guns with my faith, so to speak."

"That surprises me," he says, wiping crumbs from his top.

"Yeah... I mean I get it. They're trying to look out for me. They're concerned about my future and all that, but I feel like they're discouraging me from being true to myself. It's not easy."

"It doesn't sound easy," he says, edging a little closer to me on the carpet. He puts out his hand in my direction, then slides it back again.

I toy with how much to tell Abdi of the latest. I can't tell my family as I don't want them to pounce into we-told-you-so mode, which I'm pretty sure they would. It doesn't take me long to decide. "I tried to buy something on my parents' Bi-pay today and I couldn't. My account has been blocked. It must be something to do with the same reason I've been rejected from uni and the same reason I've been banned. The curtains are coming down on me. I'm experiencing the restrictions that Section 44 warned would happen."

Slowly, Abdi reaches out a hand and pats mine. It's like he's figuring out how to react. "I'm so sorry, Sathya. I can't believe in a country like ours which's always believed in free speech that this crazy stuff is happening. What a mess."

Abdi shuffles back on the floor, and his dark skin reddens. He gives me a prolonged look, and a pang of realisation hits me. This guy actually fancies me! I don't know how I could have been blind to it for so long. I recoil almost instinctively to avoid his gaze.

"I really want to be able to help you with this somehow," he says. "I care for you, Sathya, more than you know. I fancy the hell out of you – there I've said it now, but I don't want to mess around with you like so many boys do with girls. I'm serious about you. Would you consider saying the Shahada for me?"

I can't meet his eye right now, I just can't. My heart races and my hands are clammy. This can't be happening to me. I'm trying to discern my emotions right now, and I am struck with both how angry I am and how wrong it seems to be angry with a friend who is expressing his feelings for me.

Eventually, I lift my head. Abdi's sitting a little further away from me now, and he's turning his wristwatch one way then the other, his cheeks still redder than normal. I can't mess with him. I need to tell him exactly how it is. I shake my head slowly. "No, just no, Abdi. I can't believe that you could... get me so wrong. I'm never going to say the Shahada. It's not about you, it's totally against my beliefs. You know that, surely!"

"I know that you're passionate about your faith, but I figured that it was just the next step to take..."

My stomach is twisting and knotty. I am flabbergasted. I

67

thought I knew this guy, I thought he was safe. My good friend. Bile rises to my throat. "You're implying that my faith is an inferior version of yours, that I just have to 'progress' up the ladder of faith and everything will be hunky dory! Well, it may be good for you, Abdi, but... I'm sorry, I don't return your feelings in that way, and it would be so wrong!" I'm trying hard to keep my voice calm, but it's impossible. How can he possibly expect me to proclaim that Mohammed is God's messenger (for that's what the Shahada is) when I don't believe it?

His face plummets and my compassion rises to the surface. He stands up and puts a hand on the banister. "Well, I'm sorry I got it so wrong, Sathya. I'll leave you to it then."

I put out a hand, then pull it back again. Can't be giving him missed messages. "Can't we just stay friends? You'll find a great Muslim girl one day and you'll be thankful I said no." Even while I'm saying let's stay friends, I know that it's going to be awkward after this.

Shoulders slumped, he walks down the attic stairs, and I follow behind him slowly. I wish we could just rewind this whole sequence back and that we'd never had this conversation. But... would that make his feelings vanish? Probably not. This would still have come up in some way, somehow.

"See ya," he says, waving at me disconsolately. It's obvious he doesn't want me following him all the way down to the front door, so I stand on the landing, clutching the banister and watch him leave.

"Bye!" I finally call out in a strangled voice. "See you at school."

The front door thuds below, and almost immediately Naomi pokes her head out of her room. "I thought I heard Abdi heading downstairs. You've been upstairs less than twenty minutes. Is

68

everything ok?" Naomi has a genuine air of concern. The skin around her nose has wrinkled in that endearing way she has.

Somehow, if I offload on her, I imagine it will patch the rift between the two of us.

Following Naomi into her bedroom, I slump down on her bed with a sigh. The distinctive smell of gardenia reed diffuser reminds me of how long it's been since I've crashed in Naomi's room. Naomi goes to her bedroom window and looks outside. "Abdi's hanging around like a lost sheep at our gate," she tells me, then lets her curtain fall.

"Give it a minute or two. He won't stay long," I say, a crushing weight on my heart.

Naomi lingers near the window for a bit, then opens her curtain again to have another peek. "You're right. He's gone." She comes and sits next to me on the bed, using her knees to pull a cushion close to her chest. "So, are you going to tell me what's happened?" she asks softly.

"Abdi told me that he fancies me, and that he wanted me to say the Shahada for me."

Naomi is quiet. Her silence champs on the bits, urging me on. She raises her eyebrows waiting for me to continue.

"I don't feel the same way at all, and I said I couldn't do it."

Naomi makes an exasperated puffing sound. "If you want my opinion..."

I suddenly realise I don't, but I've invited it now. I alter my position against the wall to avoid numbing my spine.

"Anyone could see that he's fancied the pants off you a long time," she continues.

"I never saw him as anything but a friend," I protest, licking my dry lips.

Naomi turns her head away momentarily, then faces me

69

again. "He's a great guy. You could do a lot worse than him."

"Of course he's a nice guy. It's why I've been friends with him for so long. I couldn't throw away my beliefs on a romance with him, though. It doesn't make any sense."

"Did he try to force himself on you or anything?"

"Not at all. He's very respectful, but I can't compromise – you know that, Naomi."

She snorts. "I know it too well, Sathya. All I can say is you're in danger of losing everything that's dear to you with your stubborn faith."

Her words are like a blade cutting through steel. I was a fool to think that telling Naomi would mend things between us. If anything, it's worse now than it was before. Hot tears prickle in my eyes, and I can't resist a dig at her as I leave the room. "If you like him so much, you have him. I've got to get my work done." My voice is cold enough to freeze the tropics. No matter what she throws at me, am I supposed to lie back, throat bared and take it? Is that the godly way or the foolish way?

Chapter 11

The Masemi living room hums with warm chatter, the occasional burst of laughter and soft indoor lighting. It's Wednesday evening, which means church night. According to the rota, it's the Masemi's turn to host the meeting. I've always loved being at the Masemi's, as it's like a second home for me. In fact, currently it seems a safer, more welcoming place than my own home.

But tonight, I sit quietly in one corner. I've not taken the initiative to speak to anyone, though I force a smile on my face whenever anyone looks at me. A hollow sickening feeling sits heavy in me, a reminder of the worst that life has catapulted in my direction the past couple of days. Of course, Taila is having none of it. From the doorway where she's standing with her dad and Angus, she throws me a concerned look and heads in my direction, where she promptly plonks herself down on the sofa next to me. "Hey Sathya, I can tell by that grimace of yours that you're not in a great place," she murmurs to me.

"Grimace? Hardly!" I protest, then turn it into a chuckle. She's always able to lift my spirits.

"Will this help?" she asks, handing me a hard object, small enough to fit inside my palm.

It's the portable GPS. I'd completely forgotten about that amidst all the other crazy things going on.

"Thanks. It's a weird situation. I don't exactly know what I'm going to need it for, but I'm trusting it'll help in some way!" I slip it into my jeans pocket.

"We're breaking into small prayer groups later today so you can share properly then. In the meantime, we're going to eat."

Helped by a few others, Mayeso circulates the room, handing out plates of food. "Talepia fish!" I gush, my mouth watering as Marlene hands me a plate and a fork.

"It's one of my favourites too," Marlene comments, before moving along to the next person in the room with a second plate.

I love the fact that we always eat multi-cultural food in our church. There's no pandering to the dominant culture. The fish is served whole alongside a glutinous, white pile of cornmeal and stewed okra with tomato. It's not aromatic like Indian food, but the flavours are immense all the same. Mayeso always cooks with plenty of garlic, seasoning and who knows what else, so momentarily, I'm lifted above my oppression into a heaven of tastes and textures.

The clattering of plates and scraping of food scraps is the indication that things are segueing through to Bible study time. Sitting with one ankle balanced on the other knee, Angus appears to be rifling through notes on his tablet. Finally, he clears his throat and stands up. "You'll all be pleased to know that tonight's message is a short one," he says in his self-deprecating way. The chatter and clatter in the house gradually decreases, and those roaming around settle down to listen.

"Give over, love. You're going to keep us up all night," a short, plump woman cracks. The room fills with good-natured laughter and Angus' face crinkles under his beard.

"Not all night, just till 11pm," Angus responds, before swiftly moving to business. "We're continuing with our talks on Stories from the Margins today. Has anyone read the book of Ruth?"

About half the people in the room raise their hands.

"If you've not read it, it's a rollicking good read. I'm not going to read all four chapters now, but will take you on a ride through the main themes and events. Do make time to read it for yourselves though – it's well worth it. So, what do you folks know about the person of Ruth?"

"She was a Moabite," I say. I only read the book a couple of months ago, so it's fresh in my mind.

"Right," Angus responds and looks at the next hand.

"She was a widow."

"Yes. Both of you have cracked the nail on the head. As well as being a woman and a Moabite (who were a despised people group to the Israelites), she was a widow. Does anyone know why widows were so vulnerable at that time?"

"Because husbands had all the legal power at the time," Taila offers.

"Absolutely, and being a widow often meant being taken advantage of, being ignored and being poverty stricken. It's one of the reasons why caring for the orphan and the widow is so frequently mentioned as a justice issue in the Bible."

Moving away from questioning, Angus shifts into storytelling mode, telling the story of Ruth and her Jewish mother-in-law Naomi when Naomi returned to her homeland after losing her husband and her two sons. As a Moabite woman, Ruth had no reason to go to the land of Judah, other than loyalty and love for Naomi; in fact, Naomi's other daughter-in-law, a woman called Orpah, returns to her family rather than face the difficult journey to an unfamiliar land.

Ruth then takes the initiative to work in the fields of a wealthy relation of Naomi's husband, a man called Boaz. He notices her and takes her under his wing to protect her from the unwanted attention of other men working on the land. Then, on the advice of Naomi, Ruth goes to lie down at the feet of Boaz, which sounds strange to us in the twenty-first century, but was a way of encouraging Boaz to become the family redeemer, to rescue them from hardship. Of course, Boaz and Ruth eventually marry, and he courageously ignores the shame that would come his way from marrying a Moabite.

Finishing off, Angus reminds us, "This story is one incredible example of how God uses the foolish things of this world to shame the wise. Ruth was one of the lowest of the low, but because of her faithfulness, and Boaz's goodness and courage, she was lifted up and given a high status. She is also one of the few women mentioned in the genealogy of Jesus. What an honour!"

I'm curled up on the floor near the TV in the spacious living room with Taila, Marie, and a woman in her thirties called Yi Ling. There are two other groups spread out in the same room and a few groups have scattered to different rooms in the house. I'm in a half-daze, and when Marie addresses me, I barely register what she's saying. I can see her mouth moving, but it's like my ears are stuffed so tight with cotton wool that I can't hear.

"Sorry," I say, heat rising to my face. "I'm in another world! Could you repeat yourself?"

A smile creases Marie's face and I force myself to pay attention, to push through my temporary haziness. "I asked you if you'd like to share any prayer requests with us."

"Oh yes, I would." Warmth steals through the hollowness inside. It's good to be able to share with those who want to stand alongside you rather than judge you. Without fear of repercussions, I let it all out – the banning, the university rejections, the tightening controls over my life as shown by the blocking of my account, and my relationship troubles. Then I apologise again, "Sorry for taking so much time."

Yi Ling places a comforting hand on my shoulder. "You don't ever need to apologise for that. You need our prayers and we're more than happy to give our time. Shall we start with Sathya, then?"

Unashamed, I let tears trickle down my cheeks as the three women surround me, place hands on me and pray for me. Taila slips tissue paper into my hand while they pray, which I instinctively scrunch into a ball and forget to use. I'll never forget the words prayed over me that night. There's a fierceness that fires up the warrior spirit in me.

"I pray for boldness and courage for Sathya. Lord, give her strength to rise above the challenges she's facing, to know when to stand firm and when to be still and trust in God. I'm reminded of the passage in Hebrews when it talks about being surrounded by a cloud of witnesses and running with perseverance the race marked out for you, and I sense this verse is for you at this time. You might feel alone at times in the days to come, but you're not. There's a whole crowd of believers in heaven and on earth today cheering you on. Hold on to that truth!" Through my closed eyes, I can tell that Li Ying's voice is trembling with emotion. I open them slightly and see that her own cheeks are wet with tears. I've learnt over the years

75

that this kind of emotion is not fake at all; it's caused by the welling up of the Holy Spirit in people's hearts.

When the praying has finished, Marie presses me again about the GPS. I am able to tell her, "I've got one, thanks for asking. I should be freaked out about what this means, but it's encouraging to know that you're all for me at this time."

At the end of the meeting, Pastor Daniel offers to give me a lift back home.

"It's ok," I say. "It's only a five-minute walk from here and I do it all the time."

"Well, if you're sure," he says.

"I'm sure," I say, smiling at him, a new courage in my heart. "I'll probably hang around a bit longer here anyway to talk to the Masemi's. I'll bug them for as long as they'll have me."

Mayeso chuckles in the infectious way he has and gives me a gentle pat on the back. "You can bug us for as long as you like – until we lovingly kick you out!" he says. I burst into laughter and, while the rest of the group head out of the door, I settle down with Taila, Mayeso and Aaron in the kitchen where we drink hot chocolate and banter about everything and nothing. It doesn't seem to matter that Aaron's only eight, he always stays up till the rest of the family go to bed.

It's 10:30 before Mayeso starts yawning and says, "It's best for you to get going, Sathya. I can walk you home. None of this independence malarky, Sathya. I'm not comfortable letting you go by yourself."

"I've done it tons of times before," I say. "Honestly. I'd rather."

He frowns at me.

"I tell you what, when I get home, I'll message you straight away to let you know I'm safe then you don't have to worry about me."

"Well, ok then," he says reluctantly, making a clicking noise with his mouth.

The cold night air feels fresh on my face. I have to brush past scratchy, low-hanging branches that would have been heavy with foliage if it'd been later in the year. Clearly they need cutting back, but I love it when our streets are pregnant with the potential of life.

I'm halfway home approaching a secluded junction overhung with drooping evergreen trees, when I become aware of the gentle hum of an electric vehicle behind me. I glance back to see a white van pulling up slowly behind me. I'm not imagining it. It is stopping. My first thought is – it's stopping here because the driver lives in the area. The van door slides open. I can't look back again as I don't want to appear afraid. A shuffle of bodies nears me. Nobody's speaking, and I am no longer calm. My heart throbs in my throat.

Forceful hands grab me from behind. I yell, but my sound is quickly muffled by another hand pressing down hard on my mouth. I bite on the fleshy part of the hand, and I hear a man swearing under his breath. He holds me tightly, keeping a firm grip. My arms are yanked behind me, and my shoulders wrench in discomfort as they're bound with something rough that scratches against my skin. It must be a rope. Adrenalin surges through me. I try to kick my legs out behind at whoever has grabbed me, but they sidestep me. Someone else has tugged a cloth over my mouth and what could be a balaclava over my head, so now I can see nothing.

Several people are breathing heavily near me, and I'm being forced backwards into the van and onto an empty seat. Shhhhpppbb. The closing of the main door. The driver comes around to the front seat. Shhhppbb. The closing of the driver's door. Ddddrrrrr. The artificial sound of the engine starting, and the vehicle is moving, cruising almost silently forward. "She's the last one," a masculine voice says to the right of me.

"Yep," comes the reply from a husky female voice in front. "We're off. And, whatever happens, don't let them take off their face coverings."

Chapter 12

Wwe could be going anywhere. It's difficult to tell when you're blindfolded. You try to guess from the number of twists, turns and speed changes, and you think you've figured it out only to be proven wrong when your visual memory of a place doesn't quite translate into reality.

Although my mind is sprinting, it's flying like I'm floating in a hot air balloon. The ground of me is surprisingly at peace. I've somehow been prepared for *something* out of the ordinary. Nobody, least of all me, knew what form it would take, but it's happening.

From the number of murmurs, coughs and muffled protests coming from around me, I'd take a guess that there are no more than a dozen other people in the van with me. At least two – if not three – of those are our captors. They are wisely saying very little – in order not to give away too much, I presume. We're being taken somewhere that we're not meant to know about, but the question is – for what? That's where my thoughts go: up and down and round again, helterskeltering round corners and careening into cul-de-sacs. Is it somewhere we'll be tortured? Are we going to experience some sort of thought control? Or something else entirely? Whatever it is, all this secrecy convinces me that this is not going to be a pleasant experience. Far from it.

I have nothing with me other than my mobile in my coat pocket, a small packet of tissues stuffed in one jeans pocket and the portable GPS in the other. I keep thinking of Mayeso's request to contact him when I'm safely home, and he would be kicking himself right now if he knew where I was.

We've been on the move for about forty minutes when eventually the van draws to a halt. So, wherever we are, we're within fifty miles of Sheffield. The van doors slide open, and we're all bundled out into the cold air. Someone grips me by the wrist and takes me through a door. Several others are breathing horsily nearby, and it feels warm from the number of bodies crowded around. There's that faint echoey sound that you get when you're in a large indoor space. A door clangs behind us, and someone slowly slips my balaclava off. I emerge blinking into the light. My mouth is still muffled.

As soon as my eyes have focused, I notice the room has tall sides and high windows like a school gym. Then I rapidly zone in on our captors. Two of them are circulating the room, removing the covering from the prisoners' eyes, and one is standing at the front of the room. He's not a big guy, but he's got presence. He stands with his feet apart and his head tilted up, exposing the thickness of his neck. I can't see what it depicts, but there's a tattoo emblazoned on his neck. His right hand is gripping onto something that I can't see, and his left hand is shaking the air, as if impatient to get cracking. The other two are women. One of them is black and well-built and the other one is blond and bland featured. All of them are wearing what looks like army uniform. None appear a day older than twenty-five.

"We're good to start, Eamon," says the blond, and I recognise by her voice the husky female in the van.

Eamon nods his head and smiles at us, taking time to make eye contact with each person dotted around the room. It's so unexpected that my heart leaps for a moment, a hint of hope in an otherwise bleak situation. "Welcome to the Matrix Centre," he begins. "Apologies to those of you who were taken aback by the unusual method of getting you here – it is an unfortunate but necessary procedure. The first thing you'll want to know is why you're here, and secondly you'll all want to get some sleep before the busy day ahead."

Pausing, he looks around again. I'm standing to the left of the room and slightly further back. The eight other prisoners are standing spaced around the room. No one's mouth coverings have been removed yet and we've all still got our arms bound.

"The fact is that you're all considered reprobates as far as our tolerant society is concerned." Eamon shrugs his shoulders and mouth. "There's no two ways about it. The law demands that you have your rights taken away from you until your thinking has mended. It goes without saying that we'll take care of all your physical needs here, but you'll only be released once your mentality has changed. I'll say no more about that now, but you'll learn more in the days to come."

Eamon gives a sly look at the black woman, who's standing to one side with her arms folded. "Patrice, are we gonna give them time to stretch themselves and have something to eat and drink?"

I shift my weight from one leg to the other. I'm getting tired of standing in one place.

"I think so," Patrice says slowly and takes over the talking from Eamon. "To show you that we trust you to have a go at this yourselves, we're going to ask you to remove your own mouth coverings. Oooh, of course," she says dripping with sarcasm, "You can't do that until you've had your arms untied. Dana and I will help you with your arms but watch out that you don't lash out at any of us – that won't be good for anyone – so think twice before you act!"

I watch carefully, while Dana and Patrice navigate the room, untying prisoner after prisoner. Is anyone going to react? There's only one person left before me, and Patrice moves to the middle-aged man standing a few feet away from me. He is wearing thick-rimmed glasses and looks meek and harmless like an older version of Clark Kent. As she moves to untie his arms, I notice his face. His eyes shift from one side to the other as though he's assessing the situation. My heart skitters coltishly.

Wham! Patrice is floored, holding her nose as blood begins to trickle out. Clark Kent has thrown a left hook at her, and his whole body is positioned like a sprinter ready for action. I try to protest but it comes out as a muffled sound. As Dana rushes forward to help Patrice off the ground, Clark Kent begins to shake and shriek incessantly, before falling to the ground and continuing to jerk wildly. It's only when I pay closer attention to the ground that I realise what has happened. The floor is patterned with square metallic tiles like the type you might get in a night club. The tile where Clark Kent was standing is glowing brightly. He's been electroconvulsed!

While Dana helps Patrice wipe the blood from her face, Eamon comes forward and takes the bindings off my arms. He's wearing a pungent perfume – I think it's Homme's Mood Meister. It's strange the things you notice at a time like this.

I rub my sore wrists. Sauntering to the front of the room again, Eamon addresses us. "You see – Patrice did warn you what would happen if you lashed out." To be fair, they didn't say *what* would happen, only that something would. "You guys are gonna need to learn to trust us. When we say something, we mean it. So, on that note, I'm inviting you all to take off your mouth bindings. We'll help if you need to, otherwise you can figure it out yourselves. Remember – think before you act. Think before you speak." Eamon's thick eyebrows beetle together so that we know he's serious.

I reach my hands around to the knot on the back of my head and twist it around to the front, where it'll be easier for me to unpick it. Within a few seconds, I've loosened the bindings enough to free my mouth. I work my numb lips in and out for a while until they feel more normal. I'm itching to call out in protest, but I have a pretty good idea what will happen if I do, so I hold it in. There's a caution in my spirit. You've got to choose your moments to speak out and now is not one.

One long haired, tall woman, and a broad-shouldered young man have other ideas though. Almost simultaneously, "You....!" and "Sto..." burst out from them, followed by horrific shaking and shrieking as light begins flashing under them. Ice cold water flushes through my veins. Someone – I'm guessing Eamon from his clenching fist – is controlling the electroconvulsion in a highly adept fashion. These guys are well trained.

I turn my head away, nauseated.

Someone has jerked the back of my hair, twisting my head forward again. I'm shocked to realise Dana has approached me from behind. "Keep looking straight ahead," she hisses at me. Spray from her spit lands on my right cheek. I resist the

83

temptation to wipe it off and swallow the bile that rises to my throat.

"Ok," I say meekly. My first word spoken since being captured. A snip of will.

The three people who've been electroconvulsed gradually pick themselves up off the floor, still quivering. Stunned.

Eamon paces back and forth on the 'stage' in front of us, then stops and bounces on the soles of his feet. "The readiness is all," he says, quoting from *Hamlet* – which we studied in Literature in the autumn term. "We need to be ready for those of you who are quick to step out of line. So called 'freedom of speech' is over now – about time too if you ask me," he says smirking. "We're in a new world with renewed respect and renewed tolerance."

Inwardly, I shake my head. Resisting, denying.

"Anyway, you'll have had enough of us talking at you for now and you're all going to get ready for bed. You'll be in bed by midnight. Most days bedtime is 11pm, but given that this is your first day, you won't be penalised for the late night."

I glance at my wristwatch. It's 11:46. It's hard to believe it's just over an hour since I left the Masemi house. It feels like a lifetime.

We follow Patrice out of the 'gym' in single file with Dana and Eamon herding us from either side. A lady with purple tinged hair is standing at the doorway as we exit and she smiles at us, handing us each a bamboo flask. My heart stings as I recognise her as Lisa, the 'market-researcher'. I glare at her as I pass, but she ignores me. "You can use this flask to fill up on water, but make sure you only fill it up at the designated times!" she chirps at us.

Lisa – the smart, kind front of Mind Management. I snort

quietly to myself. What a fool I was to let myself be taken in by her. The skin at the base of my skull tightens and my whole head throbs.

A wicker basket sits next to the darkened window going up to the stairs, and there's a pile of browning bananas on the window ledge. Dana instructs us, "Put your phones in here, please. You'll get them back in the morning. Remember – we'll know if you've not been compliant! If any of you are hungry, you can grab a banana from the pile here."

What is this new world into which I've plunged? Certainly not a brave one. More like a coward's version, using force to control and sugar coating it with a few kind words and bananas.

My heart plummets. I was going to message Taila to tell her what's happened, but now there's no chance. They're bound to put some sort of tracking app in our phones. It won't be safe to use them at all after this. I'm grateful for the portable GPS in my pocket and doubly thankful to God for the timing.

The corridors and stairs gleam with polish and reek of disinfectant. At the top of the stairs, Patrice takes us four women to the left and Eamon takes the five men to the right. Patrice directs two women into one room, and me and the tall, outspoken woman into another. It's dark as people are already asleep, but Patrice turns on a dim security style light to enable us to see where we're going.

We stand outside our rooms while she talks in hushed tones. "You'll find everything you need on your bunk; bathrooms are down the corridor on the right and you'll be woken up at 6:30 by an alarm. It's drill time first then showers and breakfast. You have five sets of grey onesies to wear – nightwear, sportswear and daywear alike. Don't worry, they'll be washed in between."

I follow the tall woman into our room, which is spacious and functional. There are eight pairs of bunk beds in the room, pulled away from the walls into the centre. Cupboard space is around the edge. From the shapes of people under the covers, it looks like ten of the sixteen beds are taken up. I whisper at the tall woman, "Looks like we're here, closest to the door. Hope you're ok, by the way? That electro thingy was nasty."

"Tell me about it. I'm still tingling and wobbly. Do you want the top bunk or the bottom?"

"I don't mind," I say, shrugging. "My name's Sathya by the way."

"And I'm Kate," she whispers, giving me a faint smile. "I'll take the bottom then, if you don't mind – weak bladder and all that."

"Of course," I concede, taking off my shoes and clambering up the steps to the top bunk. There's a neatly folded pile of items on the bed. I look through them. There're two towels, five onesies, five sets of neutral, body-adjustable underwear, five pairs of socks and basic toothpaste and brush. That's it.

Presumably, we need to share soap and shampoo. It doesn't look like we're going to have access to hairdryers or straighteners while here. Get over it, Sathya. It's hardly going to be a hotel experience. More like being in the army, I'd imagine.

Pushing the items to one side, I crawl under the bedclothes and close my eyes. Images of my family's worried faces when I don't come home and the confusion on Mayeso and Taila's when I don't answer their calls fill my mind. But it's not long before exhaustion drags me into a deep, dreamless sleep.

Chapter 13

Drrrrriiiiiing!!! The alarm jolts me bolt upright, and I blink at all the stretching, yawning bodies around me.

"Get moving!" an athletic-looking woman in her late forties on the opposite bunk says in a kindly way to me as she leaps down her steps, "We've got to be out on the sports pitch in five minutes."

"That's all?"

"Afraid so. No need to change. Just wear what you were wearing last night. You can change after your shower."

Within minutes, we're jogging in line down the corridor, down the stairs, left through a bi-part swinging door and out of a fire door, once again making me think this is a disused school building. Dana and Patrice bark, "Go, go, go!" at us from either side, men and women alike.

We're outside, jogging towards a frost covered concrete pitch. I can't figure out where we are geographically as the land is surrounded by tall pine trees on all sides. No hint of a church spire or any other buildings in the vicinity. I stare up at the hazy sky and the limp early morning sun and bounce from side to side to keep my feet warm.

"You won't feel cold for long," the athletic woman whispers to me from my right.

At a guess, there are around eighty to a hundred people outside on the pitch. We're all wearing the same grey coloured outfits, with the emblem of a T inside a circle on the front.

I can't see him well as I'm near the back of the group, but I recognise Eamon from his voice, which is magnified over the sound of a speaker. "C'mon, c'mon – form eight straight lines with two arm's length between each of you. Get cracking guys! For those of you who are new, you'll soon pick up the routine. We don't make it hard for you," he says before bursting into laughter. I would have found his laugh sexy if it weren't for – well, everything else.

We're jostling into place, holding arms out at either side to check for distance, while Eamon barks, "Get moving, we haven't got all day!"

First thing we're doing is running up and down on the spot to the count of fifty, pulling our knees up as far as we can. Next, we're down on the floor doing push ups. Despite being sporty, push ups have never been my strong point, and every muscle in my body is straining under the effort after twenty moves. And still Eamon counts: "Twenty-one, twenty-two, twenty-three, twenty-four, twenty-five, and finish!"

I collapse in a heap on the ground, my body shaking, my heart pounding in my ears, my hands sore from the weight of my body and the roughness of the surface. If I'm fit and healthy and still struggling, I dread to think how some of the other newbies are coping.

A hard whack on my backside. "Get up!"

I raise my head and hoist myself painfully off the ground. I narrow my eyes at Dana's back as she moves away from me and watch her circulating and kicking other collapsed people. Everything in me wants to protest – to yell and shout at the unfairness of it all – but I sense it won't help the situation right now. I bite down hard on my lip to prevent me reacting instinctively.

Then, we're up on our feet again doing fifty-star jumps. I am on autopilot now, jumping, stretching out my limbs, trying not to get the rhythm wrong. Finally, we're lined up in groups of five to run twenty laps around the pitch. After the first lap, the lady in her sixties who I'm running alongside crumples beside me, her legs giving way beneath her. I slow down and take hold of her arm. "Do you want help getting up?" I ask.

"Just leave me," she breathes with the remaining energy in her body.

"I can't," I say, before I see Patrice coming close to us. Her leg jerks out, and her steel capped shoes kick the woman's backside. The woman's body jerks on the ground, but she can't drag herself up.

Fire rages inside. I can't think straight anymore. I turn to Patrice, grab her shoulders and shake them. "She's defenceless, you cow!! Is this your idea of tolerance??" My throat is scratchy with the sharpness of my words.

I'm flummoxed by what happens next. Instead of being wrestled to the ground, kicked and shoved, or electroconvulsed (clearly, they don't have the facility out here), a comforting pair of arms are wrapped around me from behind. Someone's head is rested against my back, between my shoulder blades, and a hand is rubbing my lower back. Almost against my will, engineered calm surges through me, dampening the fire in my veins. "There there, there there. I know it's hard to take in." The voice is soothing and irritating all at once. These people will do whatever they can to get compliance.

I release Patrice and turn around to see who's hugging me. I hadn't even realised that she was outside. It's Lisa. She smiles at me like a mother comforting her child. I shake my head. "What is the matter with you people?" It's an expression of bemusement rather than protest.

Lisa replies, "You were hurting my friend here, and I thought you needed some comfort. Perhaps it came out of a place of pain in your own life."

My pain? Hardly. My head throbs a warning. Don't try to argue with them. They're too well trained. God knows how long they've been trained up for this work, but they know what they're doing.

While our little altercation took place, everyone else just carried on running laps. I don't want to stare at Lisa or Patrice so I turn my head to one side, letting my eyes flit from one passing person to another. "Shall I get going again?" I ask hesitantly.

"You know what's expected," Lisa says. There's a world of meaning in her words, which I don't have time to unravel. I turn on my heels and jog off. At least this is one thing that is familiar to me. I fall into line behind the Clark Kent lookalike.

By the time drill is over, we've been outside for around forty-five minutes. It's intense – especially the push ups, but I can get used to it.

I'm standing in the queue for the showers. There are eight showers for approximately thirty women. Kate is in front of me in the queue. Turning around, Kate says, "I saw what happened between you and Patrice on the pitch. I'm not the only one to step out of line then." She gives me a wry grin.

"I got the hugging treatment rather than the electroconvulsive treatment though," I say in a low voice. As soon as I say it, I realise how ridiculous it sounds and I half giggle, half snort.

Kate returns the laugh, but quickly pulls herself together. "Any idea why you're here?" she asks quietly.

"Oh yes, I'm a Christian, who happens to speak her mind about what we really believe."

"There are a few of you lot here, from what I gather. I'm a Muslim revert. I made a few too many negative comments about secular society, it seems." She rolls her eyes.

"No head covering?" I ask, surprised.

"No. That's old hat for reverts. Looks like I'm in next," Kate says, moving forward to take the next cubicle, as a middle-aged woman moves past her wrapped in a towel. Steam tendrils drift out behind her.

"At least we're not being forced to take cold showers!" I tell Kate.

"Don't speak too soon," she says, raising her eyebrows at me before closing the cubicle door.

I don't know if there are hidden micro cameras everywhere, recording everything we say and do. There could well be, but obviously we're in here for speaking our minds, so I'm not sure what difference it makes. Best not to shout too loudly, all the same.

Breakfast is at 8 o'clock in the canteen. It's traditional British breakfast – fried cultured meat (halal and non) and cereal, high in carbs, red meat and dairy. None of the brain food that has become so popular in recent years. I don't imagine having sharp brains is high on the agenda here though they do want us to be physically strong enough. The room echoes with clattering plates and cutlery and the sound of hushed, sibilant voices. After taking a plateful of scrambled eggs on toast from the surly man at the display counter, I look around the room at the long grey tables. I spot Kate but she's surrounded already. The next space I can see is next to the athletic lady from our dormitory. She's got her head down, and is halfway through her food, but she's the safest bet. At least she's friendly, if nothing else.

I slide onto the bench opposite her. "Hello," she says, raising her greying head. The wary look that she gives me doesn't quite match the friendliness of her tone. "We met this morning, didn't we? I'm Maggie."

"I'm Sathya," I say. I cut into a slice of toast and egg and put it into my mouth before continuing. "How long have you been here for?"

"Oh, around a month now. No one has been here very long, as far as I can tell."

"Right." I notice Dana standing a few feet away on my left at the side of the canteen, her hands behind her back. She's turning her head from side to side as if on patrol. I shuffle my thoughts, trying to find something mundane enough to say. "What happens after breakfast?"

"It's mind management hour," she says. "Enough said," she continues, raising her eyes in the direction of Dana.

"Got it," I say, compressing my lips into a light grimace. Her reticence is telling. "Just an hour?" I probe, for something to say.

"Yes, but there is more of the same in the afternoon too. The timetable for the day is on the display screen over there on your right. And there's a paper copy in the dormitory too. Let's talk later. We can have a chat in our dorm after mind management, if you've got any will left."

Maggie puts her head down and scoops another mouthful of cornflakes and milk. "By the way – in case you're interested in that sort of thing – those eggs you're eating are lab reared eggs. No animals are ever harmed in the production of our food."

She raises her eyebrows at me with a look that says it all. The irony of it. Animal welfare vs. inhumane treatment of people.

Maggie finishes off her cereal, drains her tea with a sigh and stands up with her tray. "I'll see you later. You'll be in a different mind management class to me seeing as you're a newbie. At least that's how it will be for your first day. You could be anywhere after that."

A chill shivers down my spine as the reality of where I am hits me.

Mind management is simply a euphemistic way of describing mind control or brainwashing. I might as well be in Kim Jong-Un's North Korea as here.

Chapter 14

"**T**, T, T for tolerance. T, T, T for tolerance, T, T, T for tolerance!" Lisa stands at the front of the classroom, leading us in a chant. As she calls out the words, she stabs the fingertips of her right hand into the palm of her straightened left hand, forming a tee. "Everyone – actions and words together, please! Ten more times."

I repeat the phrase without much emotion. There's nothing controversial about the slogan itself. We've all heard it before.

She's just warming us up.

As Lisa speaks, she points at the psychedelic image in front of us on the screen. It's a swirl of purple, orange, green, red and yellow colours all merging together and then out again, in and out, in and out. I'm assuming that this is part of the mind control techniques and try to grip onto the truth at my core. *Don't be drawn in, don't be drawn in. My eyes are on the maker of heaven and earth, and I will not be shaken*, I say to myself – an inner prayer of defiance.

The nine of us who arrived last night are all here, as are a dozen or so others who probably arrived within the last few days.

The windowless room is around fifteen square metres, which

is small as far as classrooms go. It began stuffy and hot in here, but an air-conditioning unit blows mild air out at us. We're sitting in rows like school children from a past era. Kate sits on my right and Clark Kent, whose real name I've not yet learnt, is on my left.

Suddenly, a black-haired man sitting on the row in front of me begins shaking in his seat and shrieking. "Please, no!" he cries. I notice his seat is glowing. They're using electroconvulsion in the classrooms too. Lisa glances at him with a slow pout and flicks back a strand of purple hair. He could have been saying anything instead of 'T for tolerance,' but somehow the system knows. Another chill runs through me. Can they read our minds too? Surely not. If it could, I would have been zapped already.

Continuing to chant, the balding man sitting next to him puts out a hand towards him as if in support of his colleague, but then pulls it back, glancing around as if worried he's been seen. I've seen him, of course, but I'm the least of his concerns.

We finish the first chant, and Lisa says, "Now, that feels good, doesn't it?" We're close enough to the front to see the pink of her gums as she flashes a smile at us. She's waiting for a positive response, so we all call out, "Yes!" dutifully.

"After me everyone, I want you to say: 'We tolerate everything except intolerance.'" She says it slowly and gets us to say it one word at a time to start with. Now this one I have a harder time saying. As far as I'm concerned, it's what George Orwell referred to as doublespeak; knotty language that ends up either dangerous or meaningless. And I *don't* tolerate everything. How can I tolerate lies and manipulation?

As I speak, I form my mouth into the required words with minimal breath. Enough breath so that Lisa can't identify that

I'm not doing what I'm supposed to be. Somehow, I imagine that if I don't say the words with all my effort, then I can't be drawn in, can't be ensnared. I just need to give the appearance of compliance for the sake of biding my time. Till what? I haven't even begun to figure that out, but...

Now is not the time. I need to concentrate on maintaining appearances.

It's a long hour. By the end of it, the muscles in my eyelids are twitching. It must be something to do with the stress of intense self-control. Lisa calls out breezily to us as if we've just been for a stroll in the park, "See you all at the 2pm session! It gets easier, I promise!"

I glance at Kate as we file out of the classroom. She appears as twitchy as I feel. I want to talk to someone about what's going on here, and Kate's the person I'd most like to talk to in this place. The desire to offload is like an ache in my chest.

Then I remember Maggie. I'll have to talk to Kate another time. I give her a weak smile and say, "I'll catch you later. I'm just going up to our dorm."

"Oh, is it free time now?"

"Apparently so. I don't suppose we're allowed to do whatever we absolutely like, though, do you?"

Kate snorts gently. "Of course. Whatever we frigging like."

I like her already. She's going to help me maintain my sense of humour. I want to burst aloud with laughter, but I imagine that would be frowned upon under the circumstances, so I stifle it.

"Why don't you come up with me now? I'm going to talk to a lady called Maggie. I'm sure she won't mind." I'm not sure at all, but I'm willing to risk it for the sake of friendship.

"How long have we got till the next session?"

I turn and begin walking up the stairs to the dorms. "I checked out the timetable. I think it's just half an hour before mental training."

"Mental training and mind management? Is there a difference?" Kate asks.

"God knows."

Maggie lies propped against the head rest of her bunk, her toes flexing back and forth causing the grey duvet to ruffle up under her feet. Naomi would hate that. At the thought, a pang of homesickness hits me, and I swallow hard to avoid welling up.

"There is CCTV in the dorms – it's up in the four corners of the rooms if you want to check it out, but don't look just yet, please! Thankfully, it's just a visual monitoring system so we can talk freely in here, as long as there's no one around. You can't be sure who you can trust and who you can't."

After being sucked in by Lisa, I'm very mindful of this reality. "I bet," I say.

"The main way they watch you here is through your phones. They'll take them in every night and return them in the morning. So, think very carefully about the sorts of searches you make if you don't want to get caught out."

"I'm surprised they even let us use those, to be honest."

"I know what you mean, but bear in mind they've disabled our ability to make contact with anyone in the outside world. Letting us keep them is their way of monitoring all our activity."

"I'd pretty much decided against using my phone much here anyway," I say, shaking my head. Kate and I are sitting on my bunk, so that we can be on the same level as Maggie and have more headspace. However, I'm very aware of exposure. I spot two of the cameras on my left, as I take a sneaky glance out of the corner of my eye. They're discreet enough, but hardly hidden. It's like being surrounded on all sides by invisible bulls waiting to charge. "Are you sure they're not capturing audio?"

"Pretty sure. I've had enough 'conversations' up here to know that I'd have been caught out long caught ago if they were."

"Any idea how long they keep people here for?"

Maggie rolls over to face us, leaning her head against her propped up hand.

"I've only seen two people released in the month I've been here, but then I don't think these centres have been running that long, so they're working the details out as they go along. I get the impression that we get retested and questioned and that we're only released once we've reached a certain level of acceptable thinking. My advice would be – tell them what they want to hear even if you don't agree with it. If you absorb the mind management mantras and the resources you study in the mental training classes, then you will be out of here soon enough."

"So how come you're not out, yet?" asks Kate.

"I don't know. I'm still figuring it out. It could be that the goalposts are changing. I'm hoping it won't be long, though. I'm strong minded, but I can't take much more of this."

"Why doesn't anyone try to escape?" I ask. "It's hardly Fort Knox around here."

Maggie shakes her head. "It might not look that way, but the exit points of the building are wired up to electroconvulse at any wrong move. Somebody did try to escape a few nights back. They weren't successful. I woke up to the sounds of the screaming. Honestly, you've seen the effects. It's not worth it."

Her face is haggard, as if crushed by the weight of the world.

Approaching footsteps can be heard in the corridor outside. Maggie gives us a meaningful look. Watch out. Spies could be about.

10:30-12:30 and 4-6pm are mental training. In a seemingly random way, we're divided up into three groupings, all in different rooms. There's between 25 and 30 of us in each group. I'm not with the same people I was with for the mind management session. Rather than chanting mantras, this is like being in a traditional class. There are learning activities to engage in – all reinforcing the general principle of so-called tolerance and that we shouldn't hate or disagree with anyone for their beliefs. Much of the material used is written by anti-fascist thinkers of the 20th and 21st century including Milan Kundara – "Totalitarianism is not only hell, but all the dream of paradise – the age-old dream of a world where everybody would live in harmony, united by a single common will and faith, without secrets from one another."

In the afternoon, I pick up an article that mentions a quote by George Orwell - whose work I normally love – "In a time of deceit telling the truth is a revolutionary act." But the whole thing is unfathomable. These people are immersing us in ideas that show totalitarianism is wrong and that we should all be left to our own devices and think what we like, but their methods – including torture and mind control – are teaching us the complete opposite!

The teaching methods are absent of discussion or debate. We're expected to do gap fills and word searches and copy out pages and pages of texts. The closest that we get to thinking for ourselves is answering basic comprehension questions that engage our brains on a non-analytical level. What, when and who questions only. Not a single why, how or discuss question. It's mind numbing rather than mind expanding.

Patrice is our 'teacher' but she does little other than hand out worksheets and reams of paper, and we're expected to work in complete silence.

At the beginning of the morning session, Patrice says, "If you need to go to the toilet, you can raise your hand and when I give you the nod, you can go, but you must come straight back again. There's no other reason to raise your hand or ask questions. If you step out of line, you know the consequences."

By the end of the second session, I've been lulled into a false sense of security by the quiet, industrious mood in the classroom. *If this is all that's involved, I can handle this. Just keep my head down and I'll be out of here in no time.*

I've put my notes away in my cardboard file (we've gone old school here – it's a good thing I've not forgotten how to write by hand as I've not done much of it since I was seven years old!), when I sense an urgent check in my spirit. I can only describe it as a mental prodding, and a small but distinct inner voice urging me *to turn right when you leave the classroom.*

It's dinner time so everyone will be heading towards the canteen, which is to our left. Do I want to stand out by going in the opposite direction? I'm tempted to ignore the inner voice and follow the lines of people streaming by, but as I step outside the door, there it is again. *Turn right and walk towards the cloakroom.*

I can't ignore the voice and I sense it's the Holy Spirit. There's something that God wants me to be aware of that I'm currently blind to.

Keeping my head down, I scurry along the corridor as quickly and quietly as I can, trying to be unobtrusive. I think the cloakrooms are near the men's toilets. If I need to explain myself, I can say that I thought it was the women's toilets. It's only my first full day here, after all. The room at the far end of the corridor to the right of the men's toilets has a door ajar. Heart thumping, I peer around the door. At first – nothing. The cloakroom has rows of pegs spaced out along benches like a school changing room for PE. The pegs are empty and varnish is peeling from the benches. There's no use for them as everything that we need is stored in our dorms (other than our study notes). Then I hear a whimpering from the far-right corner, and I notice him. A huge man, probably in his fifties, is curled up on the floor under one of the benches, shaking and quivering. He's biting on his hands, trying to avoid making too much sound, perhaps. Compassion wells up in me. I glance behind me to check that no one is near, then I approach him. I clear my throat to make him aware that someone is there.

He lifts his dark eyes towards me.

"Don't be afraid, I'm not here to harm you. I'm one of the new girls. I arrived just last night."

"Get out of this godforsaken place!" he says, slowly lifting himself up and making a shooing motion with his hand. "You don't want to stay here longer than you have to." He speaks clear English with a Middle Eastern accent of some sort.

"If you don't mind me asking, where are you from originally?"

"Iran. I left there twenty-five years ago as a refugee. Now I'm regretting it."

"Why?"

"This country I claimed as a safe place has turned on me. I'm being eaten alive!"

He covers his face with his arms with his hands above his head and shrinks down into the floor. Chill wind blows through me and bile rises from my stomach. Surely, he can't mean it literally?

"You can't say anything that you really think or feel, or you get jabbed, prickled, electroconvulsed!" His voice hisses through clenched teeth. "I thought I'd got away from this sort of thing, but it's come back to haunt me like the sound of my tortured mother."

"It's not so bad here, is it?" I ask, trying to make myself feel better, while the reality in front of me stares me in the eyes. "At least they feed us properly and allow us to sleep a decent sleep."

"Gaah, it's all part of the deception!" he spits between his arms, then begins rocking and whimpering again.

"Please, is there anything I can do to help you?" I ask, desperate.

For a moment, he says nothing, but continues to rock himself.

Then he lowers his hands to his lap, and peers at me, wild-eyed. "Yes, you can get yourself out of here. For someone as young as you with so much life ahead of you to escape this place will bless me no end. Believe me – it will!" I'm startled when he takes hold of my hand, plants a kiss on it, then releases me.

Nerves flutter across my abdomen. I need to get to the canteen. "Shall we go and get some food? I don't want to be too late. They might get suspicious."

"You'll have to get used to that," he says. "My name is Bahman, by the way." He's stopped rocking and heaves himself off the floor with a sigh. "It's best for us not to go in at the same time. You go first. I'll follow shortly. Don't forget what I said, though..." Bahman lifts his voice at the end in a questioning tone.

"Sathya," I say with a smile.

"Bless you," he says, placing a hand on mine in a fatherly way.

I slip back down the corridor, passing the classrooms, towards the canteen.

Thankfully, I've not been gone as long as I thought and there is still a trickle of people heading into dinner. I join the end of the queue.

Patrice notices me coming in at the back, and says, "I wondered where you had got to."

"I just popped to the toilet," I say, my voice coming out squeakier than I intended. I smile at her, deliberately widening my eyes to make it seem genuine.

Nodding at me, she appears to let it go.

After dinner, there's half an hour's break to allow the food to settle, then it's another hour's exercise. They use floodlighting to brighten the pitch as it's jet black outside. It's snowing lightly but that doesn't stop the drill from going ahead. The drill follows the same routine as the morning. Knowing what to expect this time, things go more smoothly. Finally, we're allowed a limited time to read from the selection of books in the library, play a board game quietly or watch a film in the lounge area. The only rule is that we need to keep our voices low. There's no access to live news, however, so we can't keep up to date with what's going on in the real world, unless we want to get found out watching on our phones.

It's bedtime before I get the chance to process the day properly. I can't sleep and don't want to. I need to work out how I'm going to get out of here and where I'm going. Meeting

Bahman has convinced me that's what I need to do. I can't tell a soul what I'm thinking as I don't want to get anyone else in trouble for my actions. My automatic response in the past would be to search on my phone – ideas, leads, facts – and see where my search takes me. This time, as soon as I do so, I'll be giving away clues to my captors. If I need to check anything, it'll have to be at the last moment, and I'll have to find a way of destroying the evidence.

First, I turn face down into my pillow, quieten my hammering heart, and pray inwardly. *Heavenly Father*, I pray. *I need your wisdom and I need your peace. Getting out of here is humanly impossible, but you showed me today by leading me to Bahman that you have a plan. Thank you that love me so much that you are preparing a way for me. I don't know what that way is, but you do. I trust you, Lord. Finish what you have started.*

My prayers are mixed up with all my churning thoughts about where, when, how, but I allow it to all spew out of me. God never said that our prayers have to be clear and articulate, just that we should bring our requests to him like a father.

As I finish my prayers with an 'amen', I roll over onto my back and look up at the ceiling. Someone in a neighbouring dorm is heading out to the bathroom, and as the light snaps on, a sliver of brightness forms a triangular shape on the ceiling above me. I'm trying to work out what's the logic in the shape being triangular, when it morphs in my mind into a map of India.

Immediately, one thought piles in on top of another, jostling in an effort to be noticed. Around two years ago, Mum mentioned to me India had elected its first Christian prime minister. I remember his name – Abhishek Vishnu – because Mum said, "It's a very Hindu name," with a note of disappointment. It's as if she thought his faith was a betrayal. Why does that matter? It might be safer for me to be a committed Christian there than here. If I ran back home, I'd still be in the same precarious, restricted situation as I was before I came here, and that would be the first place the Matrix crew would check. At least I have family in India.

The last time we went to India was four years ago. Mum's older sister, Namita Aunty, lives in a village outside the city of Cochin in Kerala. We spent a joyful summer in their large house, enjoying the vast tropical outdoor area and playing with her three children and the local kids. Abhishek, Nadia, and Prasoona are my cousins. Abhishek is two years older than me and Naomi, Nadia is a year younger and Prasoona is three years younger. Obviously, I wouldn't be able to contact them to let them know I'm coming, but there is something settling about having a specific place to aim for.

How am I going to get there? I don't have my passport and even if I did, I wouldn't be able to buy a flight ticket as I don't have access to Bi-Pay. Anyway, surely no one in Britain is going to let me onto a plane with my track record? What are my alternatives? Freight ship? Freight shipping is quicker now than it was in the past and because of Brexit, Britain trades more with India and other far-flung nations than with Europe. As far as I'm aware, Hull is the nearest port. Ok, that's it. At least I have a workable goal!

On the bunk beneath me, Kate coughs loudly, before settling down again with a murmur. I can't even begin to figure out how I'm going to get out yet. It looms in front of me like Mount Snowdon on a blizzardy day.

I'm not going to think about it yet... A wave of weariness laps over my mind, and I ready myself for sleep.

Chapter 15

Bouncing up and down on the pitch outside, I try to work out the stiffness in my muscles. The last time I felt this achy was when I caught the flu aged twelve. It must be the effect of yesterday's push ups. I wouldn't say I like drill-time exactly, but it's one thing that grounds me in the day, keeps me connected to what I'm used to – physical activity. I've always loved the sensation of blood tingling through my veins and muscles being stretched to their limit.

The temperature has risen by a few degrees since last night's snow and granite clouds hang heavy in the heavens. I work through the first lot of exercises on autopilot. It's easy to see how you can get sucked down the plughole of brainwashing in this sort of setting. There's a sort of hypnotic ease that comes with just going with the flow.

As we begin circuiting the pitch, I notice Bahman's stocky bulk just ahead of me. He's maintaining a slow but steady course. Seeing him from behind, I also remember where I saw him previously – he is the black-haired man who was electro-convulsed during my first mind management session. He's clearly been here long enough to be used to the expectations, if not fully compliant. Bahman turns his head imperceptibly to one side, as if he's aware of my presence, and I slow down as I run past him. A tug on my sleeve alerts me to the fact that he wants my attention. Without turning my head, I maintain my slower pace, so that I'm running just ahead of him to his right.

"Afternoon break in the laundry room." His voice is a gentle tickle against my ear, but by now, I've trained my senses to be on full alert. I can't hear every sound clearly, but enough to help me work out what he's said. To give him some indication I got it, I nod. I have no idea where the laundry room is, but observing Eamon swaggering over in our direction, I don't probe but pick up speed again. Eamon stares at me as I run past him and yells, "Keep up your pace!"

I keep my eyes straight ahead and ignore the prickle of fear skimming me. That was a close call. Unless he's planning on confronting me later, it seems he didn't notice my interaction with Bahman, just my slower pace.

The clouds burst and rain falls with the sudden force of a bucket of water thrown out of a window. I run round the pitch one last time. Sporadic groans arise from around the pitch, and Eamon shouts, "No stopping until you've done all your laps. Come on, guys! It's only a bit of rain!"

By the time we're allowed back inside in drabs and drabs, we're all as sodden as bedraggled cats. I fall in line next to Kate, who looks as soaked as I feel, with her trainers squeaking water all over the floor, her hair knot matted against her head, and her face glistening wet. She smiles at me. "You're looking great this morning," she pants, and I giggle.

"Same to you," I say, nudging her with my elbow.

Under normal circumstances, Kate would be an older sister or close friend type. There's a natural warmth between us – a chemistry. My skull tightens as I realise that can never be here. Given we arrived at the same time and she was electroconvulsed on the first day, it's highly unlikely that she's a mole. All the same, I can't share with her everything that I'd like to talk to a good friend about. Who knows what the consequences might be?

When we enter mind management at 9am, Lisa is standing at the door beaming at us one by one as we file into the room. She calls out, "Smile please! This is a happy day, the day that you absorb the full meaning of tolerance." I force a smile on my face and stifle a laugh that threatens to bubble out. *Oh happy day, indeed,* I snort to myself. The first mantra today is the same as yesterday morning: "T for tolerance, T for tolerance." We repeat this ad nauseam until the phrase buzzes around my brain like a fly pinging off the ceiling. In the meantime, Lisa continues with the psychedelic images. This time, I feel like the images are trying to drag me into a vortex, and I want to close my eyes to shut them out. I close them for a few seconds, then open them again and try to focus on Lisa's face rather than on the images. I also say to myself, *Lisa's made in the image of God too,* to counteract the hateful thoughts that threaten to thrash out of my control.

Lisa moves us onto the second mantra, which is another one we've heard before. "We tolerate everything except intolerance."

As we say this one repeatedly, my guts start to churn with a rising nausea. I suspect it's got something to do with the effect of the attempted brainwashing, but that's just a wild guess. If I'm not careful, I could vomit. To quell the sense of panic about me vomiting, I continue mouthing the words outwardly, but speak inwardly to my soul, *Lord, you are the rock of my salvation. I shall not be shaken. I need you, God.* Gradually, the nausea settles.

The third mantra is one I've not heard yet. Lisa says this with such a broad smile on her face that for a moment I'm convinced she's insane, "My belief is your belief, is my belief is your belief." By themselves, the words seem so harmless, but when I grasp the full consequence of what this could mean – that my beliefs are no better than someone who condones deceitfulness and child abuse – I want to purge myself. My head is tight and bile rises to my throat.

"What a lo...!" I don't even realise the words have come out of my mouth until I hear them. Knives are jabbing me – my skin, my organs, my bones, my muscles, my brain – and I can't stop the shrieking that emerges; I am writhing in my seat, trying to escape the pain. Then, as quickly as it began, it's over.

I sit quietly, allowing the stabbing to dull to a numbness. Maggie, who's sitting next to me, puts her hand in my direction. It seems to be an unspoken Matrix Centre signal when you want to give a comforting touch but can't. My mind is a puddle. I can't even remember what just happened two minutes ago.

Through the mist in my brain, I hear people chanting around me, and I'm following along, mouthing meaningless phrases.

At the end of the session, we file out of the room. I don't walk, I stumble like I'm navigating a jelly covered surface. Maggie props me gently under the elbow as we move down the corridor.

"Thanks," I say.

"It takes a while before you feel normal again," she murmurs. "Take it easy for a couple of hours."

"How many times have you experienced... this?" I ask her.

Maggie is quiet for a moment. "I don't want to talk about

it," she says, gripping my wrist so fiercely that I wonder what horrific memories she's harbouring.

I signal upstairs towards our dorm. "No, I still wouldn't." Maggie shudders. "If it wasn't still chucking it down, I'd go out right now, in fact."

The rain is hammering on the skylight above our heads and rivulets of water are running down the windows.

"Where shall we go then for break-time?" I ask.

"We can go to the lounge, if you like? At least we can grab a hot drink there."

I shrug. "Sounds like as good a place as any around here," I answer.

The lounge is on the opposite corner of the ground floor from the cloakroom, past the canteen. A good number of people are there, milling around, taking tea and coffee from the drinks machine, a few sitting on threadbare sofas talking and one or two with their head in their hands. I'm all ready to get a drink when Maggie glances inside and immediately steps out again.

"What's the matter?" I say, following her. She doesn't strike me as someone easily nervous, so her behaviour surprises me.

Maggie looks around. "Come," she says, dragging me through the door next to the lounge. "This is the only place I can think of where we'll be safe," Maggie says. Her cheeks are pale.

I survey my surroundings. Four man-size wicker baskets are placed along the wall facing the door. Grey onesie sleeves and trouser legs are poking out from the top of each basket. They're full to the brim with laundry. Something niggles me about this place, but I can't think why it should. My short-term memory has been frazzled.

"Sorry," Maggie says. "But one of the moles was in the

lounge. I didn't want to stay in there."

"Who is it? And how do you know they're a mole?" I ask.

"I haven't got time to explain all the ins and outs," she says, "But she's got full lips and dyed red hair. There's no one else of that description. She calls herself Tonia, but that might not be her real name. Just watch out for her. She's even more dangerous than the Matrix crew as she's pretending to be one of us."

"Thanks for warning me," I say, licking my lips as my mouth is strangely dry. "I certainly won't say anything out of the ordinary around her, but I really need to get something to drink."

Maggie puts out her arm in a feel-free gesture and gives me a terse smile. Poor woman. I think she's been through a much harder time than me.

"I'm just heading for the toilet. I'll fill up my water bottle elsewhere," Maggie says, and wanders off.

I slip back into the lounge and potter over to the drinks machine. We're allowed to refill our cups as many times as we like as far as I can see. There's no payment required, anyway. As I wait for the hot water to fill my cup, I stand casually back from the machine and look around the room. I spot a red head who fits Maggie's description holding a drink and gazing out of the window onto the field, and take a mental note.

Bahman is nowhere to be found...

A sensation like a camera flash goes off in my mind. That's it! The laundry room. It's where Bahman wants me to meet him later. My memory has returned as the effects of the electroconvulsion wear off. The electroconvulsion used here is clearly short, sharp and intended to shock more than harm. I imagine though that frequent use would cause damage of some sort, so it certainly acts as a controlling tool.

In the middle of the morning's mental training, I am completing a gap fill exercise on the topic of freedom (oh the irony), when a thought pricks me. *What happens if Bahman is not who he says he is? Perhaps he's also a mole planted to draw in 'problematic' prisoners like me? Maybe he just wants to lure me into the laundry room to take me down?* I'm acutely aware of my racing heart, even while I remain calm on the outside.

Then another still voice reminds me: *Trust the promptings of my spirit. I don't lead you down false pathways.* As I ponder this, I remember how genuinely disturbed Bahman was. I don't think that could be fabricated unless he was a professional actor. And what would be the point of that?

During the afternoon's mind management session, I consciously decide to go with the flow regardless of my disagreement with the words that are being said. This time, despite my outward compliance, I keep repeating words of scripture to myself inwardly. The battle cannot be won in my own strength by a mental tug of war, but only by allowing myself to be filled with truth. There are times to speak out, times to protest, but now is not one of them.

As the session ends and we begin to file out, I notice Tonia standing just outside the door. Flicking long eyelashes at me, she says, "Patrice has asked me to pass you a message. She wants you to meet her in the canteen in five minutes?"

No way. This is the time I need to meet Bahman!

The key is not to panic. "Can you just give me a minute? I'm desperate for the toilet." I squeeze my thighs together in a child-like way and shrug apologetically. "I'll meet her as soon as I'm done."

"That's fine," she says, lifting her eyebrows. "She did say you could have five minutes."

I head to my right in the direction of the toilets. I have a plan. Thankfully, the ground floor has corridors going all the way around the building, so if I go one way round, I can still find the laundry room without having to go past the canteen. As I head towards the toilets, my pulse pounds in my throat and fingertips. I pass through the door of the women's toilets just in case Tonia's eyes followed me all the way down the corridor. If I turn around to check that could put me in more danger. I stand inside the door for a moment, then take a deep breath and poke my head out again. The unmistakable sound of a flush comes from the men's toilets and I sprint to my right, then left through the swing door that leads to the lounge and laundry room. Now I'm in the corridor parallel to the one I just came on from the classrooms.

Cautiously, I push open the laundry door and from the corner of my eye, I see the flash of a foot coming around the corridor from the canteen. I've no idea whose foot it is, but I have to be quick. Bahman is working inside the room. He's hoisting piles of dirty laundry from the wicker baskets into a vast plastic wheelie bin that's been placed inside. He gives me a meaningful look, opens his mouth to speak, then just as I'm about to enter the room – my body powered ready to move - Tonia's buxom frame and shock of red hair turns the corner towards me. "Ah, there you are. Patrice is waiting for you." She smiles across the length of the corridor. To me it's the grin of a hyena licking its lips and encroaching on its prey.

My heart hammers so much I think I'm going to vomit. Foiled

at the moment of escape!

I try not to look at Bahman. Don't want to give anything away. Mercifully he keeps quiet. I shift away from the laundry room and say to Tonia, "I took a wrong turn. I thought this was the dining room. Silly me."

"Easily done," she says casually. She *can't* be convinced by that, surely? It sounded like bull even to me. "This place does that to you," Tonia says, her mouth tickling near my ear.

Remembering what Maggie said, I say nothing. She's trying to get me to think she's one of us.

I follow her down the corridor to the dining room. As we enter, Patrice is standing with her back to us at a table, the muscles in her back moving as she performs some hidden action. "Sathya is here," Tonia says sweetly.

Turning around to face us, Patrice responds: "Oh thanks, Tonia. You can leave us now."

Tonia leaves the room and closes the door behind her.

"Sit down, Sathya. Don't look so worried," she says giving me a slow smile.

"I'm not," I lie, working all the muscles in my face to avoid further exposure of my true emotions. I am tense with the deception of it all.

Someone clearing their throat in one corner alerts me that we're not alone in the room. 'Clark Kent' sits in the half-shadows on the right-hand edge of the room closest to the door. I glance over at him, and he stares at me unblinking. I have the sudden feeling that if Patrice weren't looking in his direction he would have signalled something to me if he could. It's bonkers, though. He's been here the same amount of time as me. What does he know that I don't?

"We're just going to have a little chat," Patrice says again.

"Victor, can you come a bit closer," she says.

"If I must." In a quiet moment of resistance, Victor stays put for a moment longer than he probably should, then tilts his body to one side and lifts himself awkwardly out of his seat. He walks closer to Patrice and me. It's then I realise he's got his hands tied behind his back. My pulse throbs in every limb – all my senses alert.

"You see," Patrice winks at me, conspiratorially, "How rude he is. You're not like that though, are you, Sathya?"

Then why am I here? I scream inwardly. Outwardly, I just say, "Of course not," and blink mildly at her.

"Both of you make yourselves comfortable," Patrice says with a soothing tone. She can't kid us, though. This is no welcoming womb of hospitality, more a cell with padded walls.

Victor and I sit down on the nearest bench, waiting.

Patrice sits on a nearby chair and toys with her hair extensions and smiles at us. For a moment, I get the impression she's about to start flirting with us. "Have you ever wondered what it'd be like to float down a waterfall on a raft?" she throws out.

If I'm honest, I do fantasise about things like this sometimes, but I'm not going to admit it to Patrice. It's so difficult to know how to play this situation.

Victor responds with a curt laugh and puts on a falsetto voice, "Oh yes and I imagine all the things I could do with my Barbie dolls too."

I say nothing, nausea churning inside.

Instead of responding to his sarcasm, Patrice's eyes glaze over and she continues her imaginings, "The raft bounces up and down on the water and butterflies flit around your head – all different colours and sizes. You feel such a thrill and a joy all rolled into one. Wouldn't you like to experience this bliss?"

she asks me, ignoring Victor.

"I guess so," I reply, noncommittal.

Victor turns his head sharply as if in warning. What does he think I'm going to do?

"You see how he panics!" Patrice trills, keeping her eyes fixed on me. "How silly of him."

Victor is tensing quietly beside me – his presence a warning bulk. Patrice walks over to the bench she was working on when we entered and picks up two flasks. She returns with the flasks and sits again, leaning forward in her chair. "If you try these drinks, you can experience the bliss I've described."

"If it's so blissful, how come you're not taking some too?" Victor shoots out.

"Oh come on, you mean you don't want to try? Your loss," she says shrugging, still looking at me.

It might be the end of me, but I know what I should do. I shake my head. "No chance," I say in a tone that makes it clear there's no room for negotiation.

Patrice pushes her lips up, then stands up and walks backwards, placing one hand behind her. "Well, if you won't try the easy way..."

The next second, the door opens and Eamon rushes in (the door slowly closing again behind him). Victor and I look at one another, a can-you-believe-these-people look on his face (and probably on mine). Eamon paces over to Victor, who stands up – a fierce bespectacled warrior – flays his legs out in a rage but is floored with one hard action from Eamon. I barely notice as Patrice approaches me from behind and a sharpness pierces my upper arm. A cooling liquid sensation floods my body. She's jabbed me! My free arm flings out at her face – an instinctive reaction, and Patrice holds her mouth with a protective gesture. I presume there's no electroconvulsion in this room otherwise I'd have had it. But presumably we've already 'had it' with whatever we've just been stabbed with. The next minute, Eamon has yanked my own arms behind my back and there's a pulling sensation as he ties my hands together.

"Just a few minutes for you to calm down, then you go to your mental training session," Eamon breathes in my ear.

I close my eyes and breathe slowly. When I open them, Victor is off the floor, temporarily subdued. Patrice unties his arms, "You're fine to go. I know you won't try anything on now. You're already being flooded with calmness." He frowns at her, but denies nothing then leaves the room, his head low. I am piqued with a pang of pity for him.

My nausea has subsided, and I feel only the hollowness of defeat, though I presume the effects of the drug are still to come.

"You can untie me," I say. "I'm not dangerous."

"Only to yourself," Eamon says with a smirk, before complying then giving me a smack on my bottom. A barrel of indignation swells me, but I resist responding. I don't want to give him the satisfaction of a reaction. Instead, I walk out holding my head high.

Chapter 16

I'm reading words on a page, but they don't go in. Lisa's voice buzzes beelike in the background, and I force myself to concentrate on the sound of her voice. I zone into her saying, "... we've got ten minutes left. Complete the gap fill exercise, and..." My mind sways out again, like a dancer being flung from her energetic partner. I hold my pen and press lightly down on paper – I must be writing something – but I swing back and forth, back and forth, back and forth.

Lisa's head enlarges in front of my eyes – like a balloon being filled tighter and tighter. I giggle, then clamp my hand around my mouth to muffle the sound.

Zany zooey loopy loo...Twiddly pop pppleeeee

I didn't just think that last sound. A childish farty noise has escaped my mouth. Kate, who is sitting next to me, nudges me. I don't think anyone else noticed, but who gives a plop anyway?

I am like the silliest kid in school, about to explode with laughter about everything and nothing. Suddenly I know – I am in, I am under. This is just the start.

Time passes, but I can't tell how much, nor what I'm doing.

Kate walks me outside mental training, gently propping me against herself. My brain tells me I'm weightless, and about to fly away from my body so it's good that she's assisting me.

Sitting me down on one of the faded sofas in the lounge, Kate hands me my water bottle. I look at it blankly, so she almost forcefully pushes the rim against my lips and tips water into my mouth. I splutter as half of it goes in and half of it spills down my cheeks. "I don't know what's going on with you," she murmurs, "But I was with a friend whose drink was spiked a few years ago, and you're acting like her."

"Really?" I ask, slurring. I'm swaying again. I'm not surprised though, nothing surprises me. What was it that happened back there? Already, a fuzzy blanket has been drawn over my mind.

She glances around the room. A man who looks like Bahman but might be my dad – the thought makes me chuckle as they're polar opposites – stands near the drinks machine with his back to us. "Did *they* do this to you?" Kate asks under her breath.

I can't help myself. The hilarity has built up until I want to explode, and it all comes spilling out in a huge giant snort and splutter. The odd thing is that Kate doesn't seem in the slightest bit amused. "I need a tissue!" I say emphasising the 't' with a playful force.

I don't know where Maggie came from but suddenly she's there, and she helps me up with Kate, and I'm being walked through one swinging door after another to the playground area where a few others mingle in small groups.

"Don't run!!" I cry out, randomly.

Maggie speaks quietly to Kate. I don't take in the meaning of the words, but they echo around the walls of my mind. "This stage won't last. She'll start seeing things soon. Been there enough times now..."

119

By around 6pm, I have sobered up. Nothing seems quite so ridiculous as it did, nor do I feel quite so dissociated from myself. My mouth is as dry as sawdust, though, and my heart races like I've been for a run. I'm not sure if it's from the fear of the unknown or from a reaction to the drug pumped in me. Perhaps a bit of both.

Bahman says nothing to me at the evening meal, but as I sit eating pasta bake, he walks past me, avoiding making eye contact. I can't help noticing sweat pearled on his upper lip and his eyelids twitching. Or maybe I'm just imagining it? With barely a moment's pause in his walking, he slides a tiny slip of paper under my plate as he passes. I'm not imagining it.

Victor sits opposite me at the table forking his food, but barely eating. He lifts his eyes from his plate and scans my face nervously. He's also saying nothing to me. Eamon stands on dinner duty a few feet away from us. So much unspoken.

A black, slimy thing slithers along the table towards me. Eeugh. Is that a slug? How vile! It's getting bigger and bigger and has eyes bulging out of its head. I try to get the attention of Victor, but he looks at me, unmoved. He's not seeing what I'm seeing. My stomach churns. It's rising and rising, and bile comes to my mouth. I stand up sharply from my seat. "Excuse me, but I'm going to vomit," I tell Eamon. How humiliating requiring the help of one who put me in this position!

He gives me a wry shrug and points to a half corridor connecting the dining room to the kitchen and says, "You'll find a large sink just behind that wall there."

Holding back for as long as I can, I rush around the corner and find said sink, and heave up everything inside me. Out of the corner of one eye, I see a man I presume is one of the chefs walk past. "Run lots of water down there, get rid of the smell," he advises, leaning towards me.

"Thanks," I say darkly. My mouth tastes sour, but at least my stomach has settled.

When I return to my seat from behind the wall, Maggie gives me a sympathetic look from her table. She knows what's going on. I can't eat another mouthful, so I simply fill my glass with water and drink slowly. The background hubbub of quiet conversation fills the room. Plates clatter, and cutlery scrapes on crockery. Victor gazes off in the distance shaking his head and frowning, and it crosses my mind that he might be having his own 'moment'.

The slug has gone. And there's no sticky trail as evidence it was ever there.

My body shaking with that strange post-vomit sensation, I stand up slowly and pick up my half empty plate, surreptitiously picking up the piece of paper too. Somebody knocks into me from behind and I almost drop my plate. "Be careful," I hiss, turning around to see Tonia's back disappearing out the door as she powers past me. I can't prove it, but I'm pretty sure that was a deliberate push. I scrunch the paper in one fist, scrape the food from my plate and place it on the stand for dirty crockery.

I need to get on my own somewhere and I head up to the dormitory. Maggie is lying on her bed already. "Having an early night?" I ask in an unnaturally high voice.

"Not really. Just resting," Maggie replies, her hand trailing down one side of the bunk plucking the edge of her duvet. It reminds me of Naomi's comfort blanket, which she carried around well into her fifth year, plucking it against the edge of her well-sucked thumb.

"Good plan," I say, simply for something to cover the silence. I sit down on my bed and unfold the paper Bahman passed me.

Try again same time and place in two day's time. Stay strong for me. I'll get you out of here. His writing is spidery and slants backwards. I pop it under my pillow and swallow hard.

Out of the corner of my eye, a dark shape is slinking near one window. I look fully in its direction and see what looks like a large hunched up chimp. The beast raises its head and looks at me. It's no chimpanzee. Its face is deformed, red-eyed and demonic. It snarls at me and scampers closer. I scream and shut my eyes tight.

A scrambling sound as Maggie leaps from her top bunk. When I open one eye, I see her right there next to me, a concerned look on her face. "Are you seeing things?" she whispers to me.

I open the other eye. "I think so..." I reply. I swallow hard. She rubs me on the back. A few metres from me, the beast is prowling around with its shoulders magnificent muscles that ripple when it moves. "It's still there."

"It's not real," Maggie says. "Whatever you think you're seeing. I've been there. You're hallucinating."

"I shouldn't be surprised after whatever they pumped into me earlier." I shake my head and cower under my arms.

"It takes time," she says quietly. "By tomorrow morning, things should have settled again. Be prepared for a rough night."

"You're supposed to be comforting me," I say giving her a weak smile, though in her own way she is. At least I know what to expect. She's gifting me truth. The beast is still there, but with Maggie there beside me, it's lost its power. It's lost its punch. I glare at the beast and it growls at me, but it's like the sound of a cat purring, and I chuckle. I stare at Maggie, blink hard and then look back again at where the beast was and it's no longer there. "Aha," I talk to its absence. "You didn't like not having power over me."

Maggie props herself next to me against the bunkbed slats. "Wait till it's fully dark and that's when the fear really gets to you."

"Do you know why you're in here?" I ask, curiosity getting the better of me.

Maggie is quiet for what seems like a long time. She sighs. "Of course. I'm a free thinker. I always have been. Always been one to challenge the status quo. A few months ago, I shared something critical on my vlog about the new tolerance laws, and that was it. Can't be more specific than that. Smuggled into a minibus on the way home from work one day and here I am. Hope they won't snuff the fire out of me, but I'm certainly floundering." A tear trickles down her cheek.

"Do you have any family?" I ask, a lump in my throat.

"Nope, well not in the sense of being married and having kids, though I have a close network of friends and wider family. Or at least I did..." The muscles around her mouth are working hard. It seems like she's holding onto her last bit of self-control, resisting breaking down.

"I'm here because..."

Maggie holds up one hand. "Please – don't confide in me. I'm sorry, but I don't want to be party to your secrets. I have enough on my plate. The less you know about others' stories in here, the safer it is."

Compressing my lips, I nod. It's hard for me to hear, but I get it. It's not a rejection of me, far from it. She's keeping protective walls around herself to minimise her chances of imploding. There's little time to mull over this. Shortly afterwards, Dana pokes her head around the door and barks at us. "Come on, ladies! It's drill time. Get moving!"

That night I lie in the dark. If I close my eyes, there is chattering in my head like manic mice scurrying through my brain. If I open them the shadows on the ceiling are giant spiders scuttling towards me grinning devilishly. I will not scream. Thanks to Maggie, I knew this was coming and know it's not real, but I can't bear it. I hate spiders. Not the kind of fear inducing arachnophobia that some people have, but still – the kind of skin-crawling dislike that made me call Dad to take the spider away whenever there was one in my room as a kid. Every sinew in me is tense. I silently call out to God in my mind, *Get these hallucinations out of here! Let me sleep!* I say it over and over and over, until in the quiet rhythms of prayer I experience a peace descending like a soft blanket of snow. Still the spiders scuttle, but they are small and fluffy now and slowly, slowly I slide into unconsciousness.

Chapter 17

Saturday 8th February. Submissive Saturday, Selling-out-Saturday or should that be Soporific Saturday? I don't know. (My English teacher always tells me to avoid using big words for the sake of using big words, but I know that the right word at the right time has power). Anyway, it's the date I decide to keep quiet, squashing all my inclination to resistance into a tight tube of containment. That way at least, I can avoid any further electroconvulsion or hallucinogenic drug treatment. I want to be clear minded for the day Bahman helps me get out of here. I have no idea what his plan is, but I know it means a lot to him to try.

During the morning mind management session, Lisa has us repeating a new mantra, "I am one with the universe, I will not resist the flow, I am one with the universe, I will not resist the flow." Instead of fighting inwardly, I try a new tactic. Ride the words as though surfing waves. Let them carry me. Don't try to resist the meaning of the words, no matter whether they're logical or good. That way I'll be under less mental strain and will also avoid being caught out by the thought police. By the end of the session, the words are tumbling out of my mouth with ease. No matter what they are, how ridiculous or false.

This is how they manage us, by making it easier not to resist their lies. Can I avoid believing them though?

As we file out of the room at the end of the session, Lisa stands at the door smiling at us as we walk out like a teacher seeing her class out. She makes a point of smiling broadly at me, and I catch a flash of something bright in her mouth. A gold tooth, perhaps? Never noticed that before. Why is she grinning like that? Does she recognise my capitulation? A chill courses through me.

Victor gives me a barely perceptible shove as he walks past me in the corridor and under his breath, he baaaas at me. A spark of anger flickers inside – how dare he? Do I have sheep written all over my face or something? How does he know what's going through my mind? That disturbs me. Maybe he saw Lisa's 'special smile'? I breathe slowly trying to calm the fire. He's been through the mill as much as I have. He has every right to be indignant. But really, he doesn't know the half of it. He doesn't know why I'm capitulating, or what my plans are for the future. I'm so tempted to give him a snide response and even smack him one, but I hold it all back and blink at him, wide eyed and naive.

If circumstances were different, I could talk to him like a normal human being, find out what makes him tick and why he is here in the first place. But they're not. I doubt we'll have the chance to connect properly. It's too dangerous.

Pivoting in my direction, Victor removes his glasses and flashes a look at me. His eyes bulge out like they're on stalks and horror fills me again. I close my eyes and breathe through the hammering in my ribs. Then reason tells me that I'm still experiencing the effect of the hallucinogenic drugs. And he's gone, leaping up the stairs two at a time to the dormitories.

It's a long, slow day. Time drags like an elderly man shuffling across the floor with a zimmer frame.

Capitulation does that to you. Especially when it's to an unjust system.

The next notable thing that happens is in the evening during drill time. It's properly cold. The threat of overnight frost hangs in the air and every exerted breath forces clouds of condensation that drift like dandelion clocks. I stand near Kate bouncing on the balls of my feet and obeying Eamon's barking instructions.

It's not long before we're running around the pitch, the gleam of the floodlights an eerie glow on our faces. Kate, then Maggie, then Victor, then Bahman, then the older lady who tripped over – their now familiar forms run in irregular rhythms around with me, one slowing up and another speeding up.

Suddenly, a few metres away from me Victor grinds to a halt, pushes against the back of his head with both hands, crouches down and begins roaring. It's a chilling sound. Everyone keeps running dutifully, but I can see eyes turned towards him from different directions around the pitch as the roar increases in intensity. Dana and Lisa rush at him from either side and they put their arms around him, soothing him like they tried to soothe me the other day. At first, he flails his arms around and yells at them, "Get away from me, will you!! Leave me alone!" punctuated by multiple expletives. I have passed him for the second time since he broke down, and am running away from him, when the swearing stops. Huge wracking sobs split the stillness behind me. I turn the corner and see Victor, wrapped in a bear hug by two of his antagonists, weeping like a giant baby. A great sorrow hits me like I've been hit by a battering ram, and I continue to run through my own blinding tears.

It's only later that night when I'm trying to sleep that I understand why Victor's emotions impacted me so. One reason is that his feelings were so real. The second is that although they were genuine, they were also deeply manipulated by the T-team, and I felt the pain of his victimhood. It mirrored my own, our own, all of us in this place and countless others around the world suffering under this system. I turn over in bed with a sigh and pray for him, for Kate, for Maggie, for Bahman and myself. *I can't do this, God. I want out! Help him, help me!* Hot, angry tears pool on my pillow. I contemplate sneaking downstairs, finding my phone and doing a search to figure out routes to India, but I decide against it. I don't want to risk leaving any evidence of my intentions.

At breakfast the following day, Bahman slips me another piece of paper, before heading to a different table. During a quiet moment, I open it. It reads 'Don't wait until afternoon break time. Slip out of morning mental training to go to the toilet. Trust me on the timing.'

At mental training, I'm sitting next to Kate. Everything in me is alert to both the hope of getting away and the fear of being thwarted again. I only wish I could have told Kate my intentions. It wouldn't do her any good though, and that helps to alleviate the nagging sense of my own selfishness. I didn't choose this for myself. Bahman did.

I'm filling in the words on a gap fill about the philosopher Karl Popper. I easily fit the words 'freedom', 'not' and 'security' into a sentence that reads, "We must plan for freedom, and not only security, if for no other reason than that only freedom can make security secure." The truth of these words drill down deep, and again I'm struck by the irony of the methods that these people use.

Patrice has a sudden coughing fit at the front of the classroom and picks up her bottle of water to alleviate her coughing.

Now is a good time! While she's slightly unsettled. I raise my hand and Patrice looks over at me as her coughs ease. "Please can I go to the toilet?" I ask.

"Two minutes," she says to me holding up two fingers.

"I'll try," I say, walking past her and whispering, "I think I've got the runs. An unfortunate side effect...." I raise my eyebrows so that she understands my implication. It could well be an effect of the drug *she* jabbed me with.

As I step into the corridor, closing the door behind me, I'm about to walk straight ahead towards the laundry past the lounge, when I spot Tonia sauntering the corridors from that very direction. No way! That's my chances of making a quick getaway scuppered. I do an about turn, and head right in the direction of the toilet instead, walking at as normal a pace as I can so that Tonia can't suspect a thing. My ears are ringing. She could come from any direction! Once I am near the toilet, I make a rapid assessment of the situation and decide to run for it. I rush towards the laundry and slip inside, closing the door behind me. It creaks gently and I wince. Bahman is waiting for me, and he puts his finger over his lips, as if in warning.

"Quick!" he says urgently. "Now is your chance to get away."

I nod gratefully, every vein in my body pulsing hard.

"Get inside this bin, and I'll pile a few more clothes on top of you. This bin will be collected shortly and taken to a laundrette."

"Oh man," I say, all in a panic. "OK!" Bahman helps me clamber into the wheelie bin. I scrape my thigh on a sharp edge as I climb over. There's plenty of space inside, but it won't be comfortable all the same. I curl up with my knees tucked in close to my chest and he starts piling clothes on top of me. As soon as he does so, I realise what the worst thing will be. The damp and the stench. Sweaty clothes are never nice at the best of times, but multiply that a few hundred times and you've got an idea what it's like in this bin. I try to breathe through my mouth instead of my nose and get a mouthful of someone's knickers. I splutter in disgust, pushing them out again with my lips, but quickly stifle my sound.

I can hear the door opening and what sounds like Tonia's voice. "You've not seen that new mixed-race girl around, have you?"

"Nope. I've been working here for twenty minutes and not seen a soul," Bahman lies.

I've never been so thankful for a lie in my whole life.

A pause.

"I thought I could hear you talking to someone," she says. She's not giving up.

"Oh, you know me. Always talking to myself. First sign of madness, isn't it?" he jests. "Tra la la la! Hey hey na." A pang goes through me and tears swell in my eyes. Bahman is risking his life. He wants this almost more than me. Why? Who am I to him?

"Ha," Tonia says. It's a hard, abrasive sound.

For a moment, I'm convinced all is lost. Surely she can hear my heart beating through the walls of the bin?

The door closes with another creak, and her footsteps fade away in the distance. I will Bahman to say nothing more to me. I can't bear it if he gets caught for my sake.

Bahman piles in more clothes on top of me. "Can you breathe?" he murmurs close to me, his voice muffled by the weight of the clothes.

"Just about," I say.

"It'll have to do," he says.

Not a moment too soon – there's the sound of a door scraping open. I didn't get the chance to take it all in, but I think the outer exit was a sliding metal door.

"Have you got a big load for me today, then, Bahman?" It's a man with a deep, gruff voice.

"Oh yes. After all that rain, there's some wet items today so it's a bit heavier than normal, my friend. I can help you push it."

"Na, don't worry."

I can feel the ground moving beneath my body, then it stops. "Oof, you're right!" the laundry man says. "Give us a hand, would you?"

"Of course."

Again, the ground moves and after a short while, my body shakes followed by a sensation of weightlessness. My guess is the bin is being hoisted up into the air then wheeled along a metal surface.

"Is that everything?"

"Yep," comes Bahman's reply.

Clang. The door of the van is closed and that's it. I'm not out of the woods yet, but I'm out of the Matrix Centre!

Chapter 18

I can hardly believe it. It's only been four days since my arrival, and now I'm bobbing along in the back of a laundry van to who knows where, but at least I'm out!

Prising my fingers into the back pocket of my onesie, I meet the compact, hard shape of my GPS. Relief floods through me. Thankfully, I remembered to pick it up after my shower this morning. The last time I used my phone was the day I arrived. It's currently laying to the side of my pillow at the Matrix Centre and will give nothing away regarding my plans. At one point, I had thought about looking up some travel details and then smashing it, but God had other plans. My only anxiety regarding my phone is what happens if 'they' try to call my parents? Would they feed them lies about where I've been and what their purpose is? Would my parents get implicated and sucked into the tolerance trap?

The more I think like this, the faster my heart beats and the harder it is to breathe under the pile of laundry. If I'm not careful, I might throw all the clothes from me just so I can breathe more freely, and that would not be good. That would expose me, leave me vulnerable. So, I turn my thoughts to prayer, and I pray for Bahman and Victor. I pray for myself, for

Kate and Maggie, I pray for my parents, for Naomi, for Abdi, for the Masemi family and...

Peace descends and my pent-up emotions of the past few days are released as tears. I cry quietly to avoid being heard, though logic tells me it's unlikely over the rumbling of the van and the muffling effect of the surrounding clothes. As my tears dry – salty and sticky against the already damp clothing – I mull over Bahman's involvement in my escape. He told me that my getting out would bless him – but why? When I first met him in the cloakroom, he was so disturbed, so troubled, that I wouldn't have thought he even had it in him to plan such a getaway. Is he mentally ill or a man of action? The two seem to contradict themselves, but both are true. Maybe he'd been thinking about escaping via the laundry for a long time, but didn't know if he had it in him to get away, given his age and mental health. My coming along provided him with a way of living vicariously through a young person. I can't be sure what his motives were, but I do know one thing – if it weren't for him, I'd still be a prisoner.

I figure I've been inside the van for around fifteen minutes now. It can't be much longer before we stop as I don't imagine that the laundrette can be too far away from the Matrix Centre. I need to psyche myself up for the next getaway. If anyone spots me at the laundrette, they'd be on the phone to my captors before I can say boo, or they might even hold me down and prevent me from getting away. No, I can't let that happen! Clenching my hands into fists, I prepare for a struggle.

As expected, the van soon judders to a halt. The laundry man heaves a big sigh and makes a stretching sound. He's walking around the back of the van now. Metal grinds against metal, and I'm back out on the ramp, or so it seems. I feel suspended for a moment, then the wheels of the bin hit the ground and I wobble under my load then stabilise. I hold my breath.

"Dave!" he calls out. "I've got a load from my recent rounds. Are we going to sort them out now?"

"Na," Dave replies. "I've had it up to here today. Soz, mate."

"It's no skin off my nose," the laundry man says, and I can imagine him shrugging his shoulders. "Done my part, anyway. Let's just get these bins into the building and we're done for the day."

"Nice one, Ahmed."

I exhale slowly and quietly. On this day of all days, I'm grateful for lazy workers. Dave or Ahmed wheels me along the ground for a few metres and I can hear the trundling of other bins around me. It suddenly hits me that I'm chilled through. The onesies are pretty good at keeping you warm, but I've been surrounded by damp clothing for around twenty minutes now and the moisture has seeped through to my skin.

Because of the dark and limited space inside, I can only speculate on the time right now, but it can't be later than 12 noon. It seems early to be finishing off at work – but what do I know about the rhythms of a laundrette? Mind you, it *is* a Sunday, and that could explain a lot.

I'm starting to get pins and needles in my right leg, which is the one I'm lying on. I'm desperate to stretch it out, but I also don't want to make any noise, so I bear with the discomfort and wait. From my hiding place, I can hear the two men (and whoever else is here) walking around, clinking keys, clearing throats and chatting with one another.

"Have you set the alarm?" Ahmed asks.

There's a pause, then the faint sound of beeping.

"Just doing it now," Dave says. "Calm down, calm down.

Don't tell me – you can't wait to get out of this dump for a bit of action?" I can hear the smirk in his voice.

"Speak for yourself!" Ahmed says.

A door clangs to then there's the scrunching of feet on gravel and the faint sound of a vehicle starting up.

Have they both gone or is there still someone on the site? I'll give it a few minutes.

Silence at last.

Heart racing, I continue to hold still until I'm certain there's No one left in the building. I strain hard to listen, but I can only hear the faint ticking of what sounds like an old-fashioned wall clock.

Taking a huge breath, I claw through the pile of clothes on me and scrabble to the top of the wheelie bin. I push open the lid and gasp lungfuls of air from the empty room. Clambering out into the dim light, I stand for a moment on the floor stamping my feet to bring life back into my dead leg.

There's a green button on the wall near the exit marked Press. Because I have no clue of the code, there's no chance I can disable the burglar alarm. Clearly, I'm going to have to risk setting it off. The best thing is for me to get away from here as quickly as I can, find a safe place outside, and then figure out my next moves.

I close my eyes. *Help me God!* Then I move towards the exit and press the green button. The door edges open and I step through, cautiously. As soon as I pass through the door, a high-pitched insistent siren begins. There's not a moment to waste. The police could be here within minutes.

There's a wire fence around the compound and a closed metal gate. We seem to be on the edge of a small town or village somewhere. I run towards the gate, put my right foot on a bar about halfway up and hoist myself over. Quickly and nimbly, I turn right and run down an incline. It seems to be the shortest route away from the town. As I run down the street, a man walking a dog stops and gawps at me, "Where do you think you're going in such a hurry?" he says.

"Er, exercise!" I splutter, ignoring the frown he gives me and continuing my headlong rush. He probably suspects I set off the alarm but is too English to say so directly.

Within minutes, I have reached the end of a row of houses and am running along a country lane. I spot a bridle path sign on my left and I scurry along it until the path becomes treelined on either side. The light is muted, and the sky is thick with clouds. Rain is coming again. I haven't got long. I walk behind the trees and find myself on the edge of a field, where I plonk myself down on the grassy verge against a tree. Taking out my GPS I power it up.

I've not used this type of GPS before, but it's fairly intuitive with a tiny screen that sends out magnified images of your route into the air like beams from vehicle headlights. You can also talk to it much like you would talk to Alexa or Google. The first question I ask it is, "Where am I now?" and a female voice informs me I'm in a village south of Doncaster 1.8 miles away from the M18. As I thought, I'm not that far away from Sheffield. If I want to, I can mute the speaker and have the answers display on screen only. That could prove useful when I don't want to be heard. Then I ask the GPS to take me to Hull Port on foot. According to the GPS it will take me 15.5 hours of walking time. I don't have any other plan other than to walk or run right now. I'll think of other plans as I walk. I'm reluctant to ask for help from anyone at the moment, partly because I'm wearing nothing but a onesie with the T symbol on it, and it's going to look fishy to anyone inclined to be suspicious. Because most of the route is along the edge of the M18 motorway, I won't need to use my GPS all the way so I can save battery life. It'll be obvious where to go if I use my common sense.

First things first. I've been too focussed on survival to even think about my bodily needs till now. I look around to check that no one is around – why would they be unless they're dog walkers or hikers? – and hunker down for a pee.

My skin protests against the cold evening air, and I quickly zip up my onesie. Not too soon. The clouds burst forth their offering and I run as quickly as I can down back along the footpath to the country road, and continue in the direction the GPS indicates. The rain rapidly becomes so heavy that it's like plunging through Niagara Falls in the wet season. Only it's freezing. I slow right down to avoid battling the driving wind. Whether I run or not, no one is going to be chasing me in this weather.

Within quarter of an hour, I've reached a place in the road which dips under an underpass. The roar and swish of vehicles on a rain swept motorway is a few metres away above my head. I must have hit one of the underpasses going under the M18. It's a good place to wait out the rain, but at the same time, I'm worried about the risk of flooding at such a low-lying point. I crouch down against the concrete wall. It's good to get some respite from the rain, but as soon as I stop moving, I'm shivering almost violently with the cold and tuck my arms around me as tightly as I can.

I don't have to think about myself for long. From the other side of the underpass, a shadowy shape holding onto a smaller shape can be seen making their slow way towards me. As they approach, I can see that it's a black woman and a girl of maybe three or four years. The woman's abdomen is distended, and she walks with a waddle. She steps inside the underpass, puts her hand against her lower back and begins groaning. Oh my goodness. She's in labour!

When her contraction finishes, she turns to me and says, "Praise the Lord. You're an angel sent to help me!"

"Me?" I say, my heart in my throat. "I know nothing about giving birth!"

"Nevermind," she says. "You're a woman, at any rate!"

The child is holding her mum's hand. She frowns at me and tucks herself in behind her mum's back.

"What shall I do?" I ask, my voice rising in a panic. I might be a woman, but right now I don't feel very together or mature.

The woman's face scrunches up in pain and she groans again. My brain crunches into gear. "Let me help you get your trousers off," I say. She's not going to be giving birth through her clothes at any rate. I might not know much, but that's one thing that's starkly obvious!

Chapter 19

"Push!" I shout, "push!"

The baby's fuzzy crown has appeared and all I can think is – it's got to come out alive. It doesn't feel like a special moment; it is what it is – raw, messy and violent. The little girl is crying now, confused about what's happening to her mummy. Neither me nor her mum can comfort her right now though; we've both got work to do.

The woman pushes down hard, gritting her teeth and gripping onto my hand. She's in a lot more pain than me so I ignore my own discomfort.

She gives a yell – almost a roar – and the baby's head slides out completely.

I put my hands around both sides of the baby's head and try to grab its shoulders. It won't come.

"You've got to push one more time!" I say, shaking with the cold and intensity of it all.

With one final groan and sweat dripping down her face, she pushes again and the rest of the baby's body slips out.

He – it's most definitely a boy – lies there on the concrete floor all covered in gunk and my heart thunders in my ears. I've just helped a woman give birth!

"Quick," the mother pants. "Open my bag and take out the black case there. It's got nail clippers and scissors inside. You'll have to use the scissors to cut the cord. Don't worry, they're clean." I'm so impressed that she's got what she needs with her, and I rummage through her discarded bag and find the case she mentioned.

I'm not sure I can do this. Oh yes, you can, Sathya! You just ran away from prison – effectively!

I remove the sharp little nail scissors from the case and turn to the baby. I pick him up off the ground and prop him up on my left arm. With my free hand, I take the scissors to the umbilical cord and begin snipping close to his body. I feel sick at the sensation of cutting into rubbery flesh. There's a reason I never considered becoming a doctor!

"Thank you," the mum says. "Pass him to me, please."

She takes him onto her chest and holds him, cooing over him. She pats his back, turns him over and he begins a warbling, crying sound. I've never felt so relieved to hear a baby cry as I do at that moment.

I search through the bag to see what else mum has packed and discover four travel blankets cum towels as well as a selection of newborn nappies and clothes. She was clearly ready for this moment.

"Here you go," I say, passing her a deep blue blanket.

She swaddles him in it, her eyes dewy with love and weariness. "Come here, Clara," she says holding out her hand to her little girl. "Have a look at your baby brother."

Clara leans over her mother's shoulder and touches her brother's cheek. "So soft," she says. "What's his name, Mama?"

"Ooh, I'm not sure – do you want to help me decide,

sweetie?"

Suddenly, I feel awkward and don't know what to do with myself. This is a family moment, a sacred moment, and I don't belong here. I stand up, walk to the entrance of the underpass and wash my hands in the steadily falling rain. It's completely dark outside now but the rain is no longer torrential. Then it strikes me – how are we going to clean the baby? Right now, he's wrapped up in all his slime. Does it matter? At least he's warm. Mum doesn't seem to mind.

I come back in and crouch down next to the little family. "Would you like me to help clean him?" I ask.

The woman smiles up at me from her makeshift bed. "That would be helpful, thank you. There's a packet of wipes in my bag. It's not ideal for a first wash, but it'll have to do for now. I'm Judy, by the way."

"And I'm Sathya," I say returning the smile.

A lapping sound makes me turn my head. I turn in the direction I came from – I think it's south – and see a brown pool of water sloshing through the entrance of the underpass.

"We need to get out of here, Judy," I tell her, my head tightening.

"My placenta has not been delivered yet," she says, her voice quavering. Clara begins whimpering again.

A sensation like ice cool water pours over me in waves. We need to do something now or we'll be trapped in flood water. Thinking quickly, I take out one of the blankets from Judy's bag. "Here, wrap this round your bottom half," I say, handing her the blanket and throwing her trousers and knickers into the bag.

"Help me get up, please," Judy says. "I'll be fine when I'm up. It's just getting off the ground that's hard."

I move to her side, place one arm under hers and around her back and hoist her up. Judy stands up slowly. She then takes the blanket from me and wraps it around her waist. "I'll hold Clara's hand, if you can carry the baby," Judy says.

"Of course," I say, taking the baby from her. He is warm in my arms. "I've no idea where we're going to go by the way," I say, my voice quivering, "All I know is we need to get out of here and I don't want to go somewhere with lots of other people."

She looks at me as we start walking up the incline out of the underpass in the direction that Judy came from. "You're like me, then," she says. We don't have time to discuss what this means. All our burning questions are going to have to wait.

As we begin walking, Clara starts dragging her feet. "I can't walk, Mama!" she wails.

"Yes, you can," Judy says firmly. "You're going to have to."

"I so tired, Mama," she whimpers. Even I can tell that she's not just being awkward. Sighing, Judy bends down and hoists Clara onto her hips. Judy winces.

"Hey," I say. "Let's swap. You hold the baby, I'll carry Clara. You've just given birth after all."

"Thank you," says Judy and whispers something into Clara's ear – a warning, maybe?

There's an awkward manoeuvring while we swap our loads. Rain dripping down her face, Judy giggles. "This would be funny if it weren't so..."

"I know," I say grimly. There's a knot in my stomach; I can't let go, not until we reach safety at least. I shift Clara so she's sitting on my shoulders. She's heavier than she appears, but I can keep going for a while like this. It'll be easier for me than carrying her on one hip. She begins singing softly to herself.

Saying nothing, we walk for another ten minutes or so in the pouring rain. I pray inwardly for a disused farm building or something similar in which we can shelter, then ask my GPS to show me the closest farm. The blue lights point us to a location less than a mile away. We're just passing a bend in a country lane a few metres from the farm, when Judy stops and says, "It's coming."

I stand and watch in horror and fascination as a reddish, slippery mass slips out from between her legs. "What are we supposed to do with it?" I ask, completely ignorant.

"I quite fancy eating it, actually," Judy says meeting my eyes.

"Really?" I say, wrinkling my nose, not even attempting to hide my disgust.

She stoops down a little and pushes the placenta under a hedge with her toes. "It'll be a nice meal for a cow instead," she says drily, then lifts her head, her dark eyes twinkling with humour.

Both of us collapse in fits of giggles and carry on around the next curve in the road. "Shh," I say at last, suppressing the final throes of laughter. "We don't want anyone to hear us."

"You're right," Judy whispers.

In the dim light from the approaching farmhouse, I spot a low hanging building with a corrugated roof on the left of the road. Approaching it, I peer inside. From the look of it, there's nothing inside but a few discarded bits of farm equipment. I rattle the door handle, half expecting it to be locked, but thankfully it's not. The door is stiff, but I shove it with my body weight and it falls inward.

The ground is dry and dusty, but at least we can be out of the rain for a while.

I lower Clara to the floor, wriggle my stiff shoulders, and finally allow myself to become aware of how cold I am. "Please,

143

can I use one of your blankets to warm up?" I ask Judy.

"Of course you can, sister," she says. The baby wakes and begins crying, and Judy settles down in the dust to begin feeding him. I take the other blankets from the bag and wrap one of them around Judy and Clara's shoulders, unpeel my wet onesie from me, throw the fourth blanket around myself and rub my body vigorously.

It's not long before Clara is asleep on the floor, her head propped up against her mother's lap next to the baby.

"His name is Moses," Judy says at last. "A good name for a baby who's been rescued from floodwater and more..."

"You're a believer, aren't you?" I ask, as life and warmth come back to me.

"Oh yes. As you are, I take it?"

"Most definitely. I'm one of the so called 'intolerants', just managed to escape from a mind control centre." She's safe to talk to. There's no way she's just pretending. I sense it in my spirit.

"I've heard of places like that," Judy said sadly. "They've not been around long. As long as Section 44 has been law, though I think some extremists were setting them up even before that in readiness. By the way, do you want something to eat?"

With all the excitement of the day, I'd not even been thinking about it. But as soon as she asks, I become aware of the emptiness in my stomach. I check my watch. It's 19:43.

"I have no money, no food, nothing. All I have is my portable GPS and the clothes I'm wearing. It kinda gives me away as being from a centre, don't you think?"

"I did wonder," says Judy. "I've got some energy bars in my bag. You can have one. There's also two water bottles at the bottom of my bag."

Contemporary energy bars are meals in themselves – a fortified, concentrated mix of nutrients including vegetables, fibre, calcium and protein all compressed into a tasty rectangle. You can get fruit flavoured ones too, but the savoury ones are much more substantial.

"You came very prepared," I say, taking out two bars and passing one to Judy. "Seems like you knew you'd be on the run?"

"I did," she says, peeling off the wrapping on her bar and taking a mouthful. "It's cos of my brother-in-law, Rashid. Both he and my husband, Yaro, are Muslims but Rashid has always hated the fact that I came to Jesus. Yaro is more easy-going on the other hand. Live and let live is his motto. Rashid saw Section 44 as an opportunity to dig at me, to undermine my position with Yaro. It's a long story, but I knew he was going to turn me in to the tolerance crew. I couldn't allow my children to go through that. I'd have been even more vulnerable once Moses was born, because then Moses would have been registered and it'd have been more obvious if I'd slipped away – three missing people instead of just two."

"Nevermind the fact that you were heavily pregnant!" I say, impressed at her gutsiness.

Shrugging, Judy gives me a wry grin. "I'm a nurse. I can handle anything".

"Why didn't your husband do anything to stop him?" I ask, swallowing a mouthful of energy bar.

Judy shakes her head. "It pains me to say so as I don't want to dishonour him, but Yaro is too weak to stand up to his brother. He always has been."

"I'm sorry to hear that," I say fingering the edge of my blanket. "Where are you from by the way?" I ask.

"I'm from Leeds," Judy replies, "And from the sound of it, you're a Sheffield lass, right?"

"Yeah. I'm impressed that you can tell!"

"I've always been a natural when it comes to distinguishing accents. What's your story, then?"

It's therapeutic telling my story to someone who can relate. I go into more detail than Judy did, telling her about the stages leading up to my capture and then all that followed. She listens to me quietly, a look of concentration on her face. When I get to the part about meeting Bahman, she takes hold of my hand and strokes it with her thumb in a sisterly fashion. I'm touched to see tears glistening in her eyes.

"I knew someone like Bahman," Judy remarks, "So brutalised and trampled on that you wept for him – yet at the same time with a spirit of generosity and kindness towards others."

For a moment I can't speak, and swallow past the lump in my throat. I'm still anxious for him. I hope that he didn't get into trouble on my behalf. It must have been obvious that he had something to do with it, once they'd figured out I'd got away – or was it?

"To be on the safe side," Judy says. "I think we need to get away from here by 4am. I have a friend who's a farmer and sometimes they're up as early as 4:30. We don't want to run any risk of getting caught."

"Of course not," I agree. "I'm happy to use the alarm on my watch to wake us up so we can get some sleep tonight. What's your plan? Do you want to come with me to Hull? I'm planning to sneak onto a freight ship to travel to India."

"Why India?" Judy asks.

"I have some family there, plus I'm aware it's a safe place for Christians at the moment – at least as far as the law is concerned."

"Brilliant. I won't be coming with you, I'm afraid, as I'm planning to travel to Tanzania from Portsmouth, but I do have some knowledge about freight ships from Hull which could be helpful to you."

"Yes please," I say, warmth surging through me. "Any tips would be great."

"Someone in my church knows a friend of a friend who's working as staff on the Govinda Line freight ships. He's known as Sabu – it might be his real name or a code name."

I make a mental note to remember that name. "It sounds like an Indian name," I say.

"It is – as is the man. He's willing to help refugees like you and me stow away safely, and will help with food and water and so on."

My heart throbs when I hear the word refugee. Refugees are always other people. It's hard to believe it's a description that fits me.

"Any idea which part of India his ship's headed to?"

"No idea, sorry..."

"It's ok, I'll have to travel within India if needs be. At least I've got some leads now, thank you."

Judy's eyes light up with a remembered thought. "I almost forgot to mention – apparently he uses a fish shaped gesture to identify himself. But I know nothing else, I'm afraid."

Chapter 20

Cold seeping up from the hard ground wakes me. Using the light on my watch, I see it's 3:31, twenty minutes before the time my alarm is set. I wrap the blanket around me even more tightly and listen to the comforting sound of breathing near me.

How am I going to get from here to Hull? If I just walk, it will take me fifteen hours. Running part of the way will shorten that time by a few hours. On nothing but an energy bar, I'm not sure I'll have the strength to run the whole way. I don't have any money so even if I want to, I can't get a bus. My only other option is hitchhiking, but it's too much of a risk. Of course, I could be raped or attacked, but that's not my biggest fear. My brain pulsates at the thought of someone turning me in and ending up back at the Matrix Centre or somewhere similar again. Undoubtedly, I'd be treated even worse than the first time if I were caught running away.

Rolling onto my front, I check my GPS data again, and I'm informed that cycling will take four hours and fifteen minutes, so probably, my stop-start running will fall somewhere between the cycle time and the walking time – around nine to eleven hours, at a guess.

We've not been acquainted long, but already there's a bond between Judy and me. It's not going to be easy to say goodbye, especially knowing she's got to get herself and two small children to the south coast of England all on her own – a much more challenging task than mine. Lifting myself off the floor, my muscles are stiff and aching. It's more uncomfortable sleeping on a hard dirt floor than I'd thought.

Clara wakes up with a whimper and begins crying. "I hungry!" she says, gulping for breath through her tears. Fumbling around for Judy's bag, I take out one of the energy bars, unwrap it and pass it to Clara with a "shh, shh." She sits up off the floor, her tears slowing down to a shudder, and gobbles gratefully.

The alarm is two minutes away from going off, but I lean over and shake Judy. She is sleeping motionless on her back, and it might take a while to rouse her.

We're standing near the underpass where Judy gave birth. There was no further rain overnight and the floodwaters have receded though there's still a huge puddle on the southern side which we'll need to navigate. I throw my arms around Judy and Moses (who's tucked into a sling on her chest) and squeeze them tight. Clara holds onto Judy's hand and gapes at me with big, watchful eyes.

"I can't think what to say regarding keeping in touch," I blurt out. "I don't have a phone, all my social media has been banned, and I don't know any land numbers off the top of my head. What's your surname? I'll search for you again once I'm in a safe place."

"Shabani," Judy says, standing back and looking at me with tears in her eyes. "Don't worry, I'm never going to forget you, Sathya. How could I after what we've been through together?

Let's keep each other in our prayers."

Judy takes off her shoes and socks and helps Clara off with hers. They paddle through the ankle-deep water. Clara jumps in with a splash then her whole body tightens, "It's cold, Mama."

"Keep going, we're almost there," Judy coaxes.

Judy is heading south following the A1, whereas I'll be heading east and don't need to go through the underpass at all.

Turning around, Judy gives me a final wave. "Take care, Sathya. May God be with you."

"And you!" I say, drinking in the sight of the little family. My throat is tight. A little tremor of longing for friendship.

I took a last swig of water from Judy's backpack before we left our hiding place. I could easily have drunk more but I am very aware that Judy is looking after three people, two who are too young to go without fluids and I didn't want to deplete her supplies. It wasn't much, but I'm going to have to get used to not drinking during the day. I'm not sure when my next meal or drink will be nor when I'll next be able to wash. I remember from a biology lesson that the human body can survive for around three days without water, so I'll be ok for now.

Taking a deep breath, I start pounding the road that my GPS is pointing me down. Unlike the country lane we took to the farm last night, it has a pavement, which makes me feel a bit safer, although it's still not 5am so there's not much traffic about, anyway. It's only mid-February – two and a half weeks since I got my university rejections. So much has happened in such a short space of time – "a whirl of days" as Mum used to say. It's still at least two hours until sunrise. I figure that the more I run in the dark the better, as it'll get warmer and I'll use more energy once the sun is up. The good thing with jogging is that people are less likely to be suspicious of me – so long as I give the impression of being relaxed and not like I'm on the run (and so long as people don't look too closely at the T on my onesie)! After all, jogging is one of the most common outdoor pursuits these days in Britain. You'll see joggers everywhere, not just in the big cities.

At first, I quite enjoy the exercise – the impact of solid ground under my feet, the rush of cool air against my face and the exhilaration of freedom. Only two days ago, I was a prisoner. Now, I'm alive and... I won't say without a care in the world as that wouldn't be true, but at least not bound to anyone or anything – except God.

The horizon is tinged with flames of burnished red, orange and mauve, and I've been running for two solid hours. The beauty moves me like the imprint of the divine on my soul and I wipe away the unexpected tears that wet my cheeks.

The stirring of heaven in me does nothing to diminish the growing dryness in my mouth and gnawing hunger. I pray inwardly: *Lord, provide me with something to eat and drink. You know my every need and I trust you.*

I might be able to survive without sustenance, but I don't want to just manage as if dangling on a thread. I want to thrive.

Slowing right down to a walk, I see a 30-mph road sign followed by a dark blue town sign with the words 'Welcome to Thorne: Historic Market Town' embossed on it. One part of me sinks, knowing that I've only run around ten miles so far. I'm aware Thorne is about that distance from Doncaster. But I'm also aware that a town means people and people increases the chance of food. It's still too early for many people to be around, but that's probably a good thing. I'm still praying for provision.

I meander through the carpark of one of the newest supermarket chains – Marvin and Mealies – and weave my way around trying to find something, anything. There's a rattling sound and my trainers crunch against something solid. Looking down at my feet, my heart leaps. It's a can of pop that's rolled out from near the tyres of someone's car. I've never been so pleased to see litter on the ground as I am now. I bend down and pick it up. Thankfully, it's unopened. Right now, I can't think about where it's come from – it's a gift for me, I'm convinced of it! The can springs open with a hiss and I slowly drain the raspberry flavoured liquid. I'm aware that if I drink too quickly, it'll cause too much gas, and I could do without drawing attention to myself in a public place. I hadn't realised quite how parched I was until my thirst is quenched.

Having weaved my way through the whole carpark, I exit and head east along the pavement. There's a fish and chip shop a few metres away on the other side of the road and a waste bin outside. The shop is closed – it's still only 7:30am after all. An attractive male jogger skirts around me as I stand near the bin hoping I can 'discreetly' check out what's inside. My face heats up with shame. Am I really having to stoop so low as this? Then, a pang of guilt hits me. How dare I talk about stooping low? I'm startlingly aware that by condemning myself, I'm judging those for whom this is a lifestyle they've not likely chosen.

As soon as the jogger's back dwindles out of sight, I lower myself over the bin and rummage through the paper packaging, banana peel and general waste. Ignoring the niggling heat crawling over me, I lift a crushed can and find a half-eaten bag of chips and a whole banana (a little browner than I like). My breakfast! I take them out, glance surreptitiously around me

152

and begin eating. To be honest, if they're carrying any germs, I couldn't care less right now. As far as my hunger is concerned, it's as good as a plate of Mum's homemade food. Necessity is most definitely the mother of invention and... indignity. I probably could have waited longer to eat, but I'm glad I was able to take advantage of my first opportunity.

It's late morning. I've been walking-running-walking-running for three hours since leaving Thorne. My legs are getting tired, but according to the GPS, I've still got a good seven hours walking till I reach my destination. The running is definitely helping me to make good time, so if I carry on as I am, I might do it in five hours. I'm now following the M62 motorway, having recently passed a town called Goole. I decided against walking through the town this time, instead circuiting it. If I keep the motorway within a mile or so of my route, it is easy for me to navigate.

Because the day is well underway, I'm now deliberately trying to avoid places where there are likely to be lots of people. It means getting to Hull after dark will be best for me as I can move around more inconspicuously. The port is on the eastern side of the city, and it looks like there is no way for me to completely avoid the built-up areas to get there unless I want to take a huge detour. I can afford to have a break.

I'm walking along a footpath with a field on one side and a grassy verge backed by a hedgerow on the other. On the other side of the hedgerow, there's a narrow country road. I put my hand down on the grassy verge. Considering how heavily it rained yesterday, the ground is surprisingly dry. The air is crisp and bright, so the sun has had a bigger impact than I'd have expected for February. I fling myself down on the grass and lie flat on my back gazing at the sky. Wispy clouds are beginning to scud across the sun, but there doesn't seem to be any threat of rain. Given how little sleep I got last night, I decide that it's safe for me to have an hour or so of sleep and I set my watch alarm for 1pm and allow my body to relax...

When my alarm wakes me, I roll over with a jerk, slamming the back of my hand on the ground. *Where am I? Where's that cold air coming from? Surely I didn't leave my window open all night...* My eyes focus themselves and I reorientate. There's no window. I'm not back home in my cosy bedroom. I'm alone somewhere on the edge of the East Riding of Yorkshire.

It's no longer sunny. There's that kind of hazy yellowy grey – like your grandma's duvet covers – that you often get on wintry days. I wipe sleep from my eyes and sit up on the grass. I need to get moving soon or I'll soon start getting really cold again.

Switching on my GPS, I ask it to tell me the departure times of freight ships from Hull to India. The automated voice asks me sweetly which port I want in India – Kandla Port, Mumbai, Navasheva, Murmagoa, New Mangalore or Kochi. I don't recognise half the names, but I do recognise Kochi – it's the Malayalam name for Cochin. "Kochi" I reply, my heart hammering excitedly. There *is* a direct line after all!

The GPS informs me that the next freight or cargo ship to travel from Hull Port is at 04:34 tomorrow morning. The subsequent one is three days later. My heart sinks. I shouldn't have been surprised though. There's hardly likely to be more than one ship travelling per day. It's not a sightseeing trip. At least it's not this afternoon as I'd struggle to make it in time today and would have even longer to wait if it were tomorrow afternoon.

The sound of giggling pierces my consciousness along with the rustling of leaves being pushed back. I press myself down into the ground again, roll down the slope and pray that the slight hummock I've rolled over will hide me from view.

I hear the faint sound of liquid being released, and a female voice calls out, "I needed that. You've no idea how desperate I was!"

Slightly further away and closer to the road, a man comments, "You never fail me when we do car journeys – and always when we're miles from a service station."

"Sounds like it's all for your entertainment or something!" the woman replies.

"Well, you know…"

"Hey, not now, Henry!" she giggles again.

"Why, you worried about the tolerance police catching us or something?"

"Not for the reason you're thinking anyway, but…" she pauses, a more serious note in her voice – "Did you hear about Livi going missing?"

"No, what happened?"

"She was walking back home from her church meeting last night and then just disappeared. None of her close friends have been able to get hold of her. Seems like she was kidnapped or something. Shocking stuff."

"It's not as unusual as you might think," the man says.

My heart leaps. If nothing else, they're safe people. I let their voices fade slightly while I send a quick prayer to the heavens – *give me wisdom* – and try to figure out my next move. I have to act quickly, or they'll be gone.

Chapter 21

I clear my throat and step out from behind the hedgerow. Henry and his partner are slouching against a dark blue car holding flasks. Despite my attempt to make my appearance obvious, the woman jumps when I draw near. Both slim and dark haired, they appear to be in their late twenties.

"Sorry, I didn't mean to startle you," I say. "I was just walking on the footpath behind that hedge."

"It's ok," the woman says. "Can we help you at all?" I clearly look like someone who needs help. Glancing down at my grass-stained onesie, I hope against hope that they don't notice the 'T'. If they comment, I'll have to tell them the truth so that they don't think the opposite.

I laugh, trying to sound casual. "Yes, you could say so!" My mind works rapidly. I think I've got a plausible story. "My sister and I have been trying to compete to see who can get from Goole to Hull on foot the quickest. Sometimes she makes the runs and sometimes I do, and we keep a record of our times on our exercise app. Unfortunately, today I've sprained my ankle," – I limp to make it convincing and hope it doesn't look contrived – "and I was wondering if I could catch a lift at least part of the way...?"

Henry turns to his partner, and they both start to speak at once. "You go first!" Henry says laughing.

"Ok. We're actually heading home to Beverley – do you know it?"

"No, I don't," I admit. "I've heard the name but am not sure exactly where it is."

"It's about ten miles north of Hull. Would that help or do you want us to drop you off in Hull itself?"

I do a rapid calculation. It'll shave off a few hours of walking and running time at least. To be honest, being near a town rather than the city will be easier for me as I can hang around outside the town while waiting for the right time to move on again without being too near random strangers. "I'm quite happy to come to Beverley with you. I don't need to be back in Hull until at least eleven this evening. My sister doesn't finish her bar job until then, so I'm in no massive hurry."

"Great. Hop into the back then," she says smiling broadly at me. "By the way, I'm Annie and this is my husband, Henry." Annie holds her hand out for me to shake.

"I'm Sathya," I say, shaking her hand. This is one thing I can be honest about. They don't know me from Adam and the name alone will hardly connect me to the Matrix Centre, I don't think so anyway...

Doubt stings me as I get into the backseat of their car. Maybe I should have introduced myself as Sarah or something similar instead? I probably shouldn't let my guard down until I reach India. They seem to be safe people, but I don't want to tell them too much all the same. It's not worth the risk to me or to them.

Henry gets into the driver's seat and Annie sits next to him. Henry starts up the engine and we drive off. It feels good to be inside away from the cold for a while, and I enjoy the warmth on my skin as the car heater starts up. "It shouldn't take us more than half an hour to get home," says Henry. "Sit back and relax."

That's twenty miles of time and energy saved for me. I'm very grateful. Within minutes, we slip onto a flyover and up onto the motorway where we're soon flying along at 70mph. Annie turns around and chatters to me from the passenger seat.

"Henry and I are quite competitive too. A few days ago, we took part in a cycle challenge along the east coast. I managed to beat him by 5 minutes. He's still smarting about it now!"

I watch Henry frown in the driver's mirror. He gives Annie an elbow dig. "Only when you make comments like that. Cool as a cucumber otherwise."

"My sister and I are like that too. I'm more sporty, but she's definitely more competitive. Can't stand to lose!" It feels good to engage in banter with normal people, even though I'm also aware of the need to zip myself in to avoid too much mess spilling out.

When a road sign indicates that we're only seven miles away from Beverley, Annie turns around to talk to her husband. "What's our plan for this evening?"

"I was thinking we could eat out then go out for a drink or two."

"How about we eat in today and Sathya can hang out with us until the time she needs to get to Hull? It'll give her something to do and give us some company."

"Er, yeah, why not, if she'd like ... or you can come out with us instead?" Henry asks, looking at me quizzically in the mirror.

Going out in a public place with too many people around would *not* be a good idea. You have no idea who might be around spying out trouble. "Staying in would be nice. Thank you so much," I say. Then, because I have this sudden urge to explain myself, I add, "I get bored with eating out too often," and grin goofily. If I say I've not got any money, they'll offer to pay for me and that won't solve the problem of other people!

"We can get in some takeaway..." says Henry then after a pause. "Hey, what was that for?" I think she gave him a punch or something.

"It's ok, Henry. I'm more than happy to cook," Annie says, smiling then rolling her eyes at me as if to say 'men'!

Not wanting to collude with her in their little conflict, I turn my eyes to the window, and smile to myself. Not only have I saved hours of walking time, but I'm also being treated to a proper meal. What could be better?

It turns out that Annie and Henry live in a cosy flat on the top floor of a Georgian house near Beverley's understandably famous minster. I'm not the biggest fan of old buildings, but even I was impressed by its vast, beige gothic spread as we approached it twenty minutes ago.

"You don't mind if I catch up on a couple of hours sleep, do you?" I ask Annie as she comes into the lounge with a tray of hot drinks and biscuits. Having the opportunity to relax after all the adrenalin has made me realise just how exhausted I am, and who knows when I'll get the chance for some proper rest again?

"Not at all," Annie replies, her eyelids blinking at me rapidly. "We won't be eating until around six, so you've got plenty of time. Finish your coffee and biscuits then you can take a nap in the spare bedroom. Feel free to take a shower as well if you like."

"I stink, right?" I ask, making a joke of it.

"Not at all!" she repeats, but I'm pretty sure she's just being polite.

The problem is I don't have any clean clothes to change into. "I don't suppose I could borrow a dressing gown or something and I could clean and dry my onesie?"

"I don't have a dressing gown," Annie says, "But I can lend you some trackie bottoms and a t-shirt. We don't have a spin-dryer but we've got a portable clothes dryer that'll dry clothes within half an hour."

"I'm happy to hand wash to save you energy," I say.

"No worries. I can make up a full load anyway with our stuff. You'll then be nice and clean for your meeting with your sister."

"I really appreciate your help," I say, taking a sip of my coffee.

It's a funny thing that when your body most needs rest, your mind is frequently most active. As soon as I lie down to sleep, my mind kicks into gear. The truth is that I have no idea how I'm going to connect with Judy's contact – Sabu – and get on board the ship unseen. Lots of stuff has just 'happened' to me, like Bahman helping me escape, but I have a feeling that I'm going to have to be more proactive in my planning than I have been. There's a device on the wall in my room. They've been so accommodating; I'm sure Annie and Henry won't mind if I check the internet. Caution warns me if I do that, they might be able to track my plans. Then it hits me that it really doesn't matter. They're unlikely to care or to even check up on my browsing history.

I sit up in bed and wave my hand near the device. It might be fingerprint protected, in which case I'm stumped. Thankfully it's not and I'm able to connect. I don't want to put on any videos as they'll hear me, but I look up some images of the layout of a cargo ship and discover that the accommodation is in a building called the superstructure in the stern of the ship and the containers are placed like Lego bricks one on top of each other in the bulk of the ship. I can't imagine it'd be safe to stow away in an airtight container for all that time. My mouth gets dry as I start thinking about the reality of the danger I could be in. Cargo ships are quicker than they used to be, but being holed up for even fifteen days is going to be hard. I almost wonder if I should have decided to fly instead, but without a passport, it would be impossible. Hopefully, I'll be able to stow away in a cupboard or something like that.

The main thing is – I don't want to be caught. Finding Sabu is imperative to my success, and that's something I can't easily plan for as I don't even know if he'll be there. My head spinning, I turn off the device and pray feverishly for God to help me find Sabu. It won't be as simple as just keeping an eye out for the 'Indian man' as there is likely to be more than one of them on a ship headed towards India! In the stampede of my mind, a still space opens up and I sense the Spirit impressing on me the words, 'Trust in me' and 'Be alert'.

At the end of the day, there's no certainty in circumstances. If there were, where would be the need to trust?

Chapter 22

"**Y**ou were sleeping so deeply, I was reluctant to wake you," says Annie, ladling beef stew onto my mash.

"I could have slept for hours," I say, before quickly changing the subject: "This looks amazing." I'm salivating at the sight of the food. There are fresh coriander sprigs on top of the stew, and I'm sold already.

"Oh, it's nothing," she says with a shrug of her lip. "It's a family favourite – a go-to comfort dish."

"She says it like it's so easy, but she spends hours slaving over this dish," Henry comments, swallowing a mouthful and giving me a cheerfully watchful expression. "She loves it though," he says, turning to Annie with a wink.

"Hardly slaving," Annie rebukes. "Be careful with your words, Henry..."

I'm tucking in, wanting to make the most of what could be my last decent meal for a long time. My mouth full, I give the couple a contented grin and a thumbs up.

As we sit eating, for a moment I'm tempted to open up and tell them everything. Their generosity has been like ointment on a wound. Sathya means honesty and it's always been against my nature to deceive. However, I have to rein in my inclination to spill my soul as it won't help any of us. I am reminded of an incident in Corrie Ten Boom's story told in *The Hiding Place* where her and her family are hiding Jewish people in their house in Holland, and they lie to the Gestapo about their whereabouts. The deception was not a run-of-the-mill thing: it was done to save precious lives. Am I facing a similar situation a hundred or so years later? It's not life or death exactly, but it could be – in some circumstances. We just don't know enough about the dark side of the tolerance agenda yet, and it's not worth the risk.

"You're very quiet," says Annie.

"I'm not usually," I say, "But your food is so good!" Even though that's only part of the story it's still true. Depth requires openness and I'm sad that I can't connect on a deeper level with these kind people.

"I hope you don't mind me saying, but we noticed the 'T' on your onesie. Is everything ok? You can talk to us – if you like." Annie moves her hand out across the table towards me. My heart flips like a pancake. This could be my opening...

No. Despite my previous conviction that if they asked me about the 'T' I would tell them the truth, I've changed my mind. I'm not going there again. Being too open was my downfall with Lisa.

"Oh, that's T for Taila. My best friend is called Taila and for Christmas one year we bought each other onesies with our initials on – one of those girly things!" I laugh flippantly. A muscle is twitching near my right eye though and I hope they don't notice it.

"Ok, no worries. We were just wondering..." Annie replies, giving me a quick tight smile. "We're aware of some people who've been badly affected by the tolerance agenda, but it's good to know that you're not one of them." I'm pretty sure she doesn't believe me.

My heart is hammering again – it's like that feeling you get just before you vomit, but without the bile. Resisting is harder than I thought it would be. Thinking rapidly, I decide the best thing is for me to get out of here as soon as I can without being rude.

"Hey, you guys have been absolutely amazing, but I'm thinking it'd be good to get out of your hair soon and head to Hull."

"How were you planning on getting there?" Henry asks.

"I was going to run, but," – I remember I'm supposed to have a sprained ankle – "I think it's more likely going to be a walk!"

"Well, it depends on your time frame. We'd be happy to give you a lift there, if you like? Unless you really want to walk of course!"

"My GPS tells me it'd take me around two and a half hours to get to Hull on foot. It might take a bit longer considering my ankle... so it'd be best for me to start around 8pm, I'm guessing."

Annie looks at Henry with a frown, then Henry turns to me decisively and says, "Nope, sorry, we're not letting a young woman walk three hours on a hurt ankle. We'll give you a lift. We can hang out together and watch a movie or something beforehand."

"Yeah, I think that's best, Sathya," Annie says giving me a compassionate smile.

"Great. I'm not going to complain about that!" I grin. Watching a film is perfect as it'll avoid me having to talk too much.

It's 22:45 and I'm sitting at the front of the car with Henry, heading southeast towards Hull. Outside, the lights from other vehicles illuminate the darkness, and I watch the almost hypnotic movement of cars flashing by. I've not said a word since leaving Beverley and Henry is less talkative without Annie, so we've sat in companionable quiet with only the sound of the radio in the background.

"Where do you want me to drop you off, exactly?" he asks as we enter the suburbs.

I'm not familiar with Hull, but I have prepared for this question at least. I don't want him to take me too close to the port. I'd rather walk from somewhere central. So, I've plumped for, "Drop me off somewhere near Princes Quay. My sister works near there." It's about three miles from there to the port, but I don't want Henry to get suspicious. After all, I did say my sister was working in a bar.

My stomach is churning. The closer I get to leaving the country, the more nervous I feel about getting caught.

After a few more minutes, Henry pulls in the car a few metres away from a shopping centre. It's a short walk along a pedestrianised road to get there. "Take care of yourself, Sathya, and do let us know if you are heading our way at any point."

"Thanks, I will do. I really appreciate all your kindness today. It means a lot to me." There's a slip of paper with Annie's mobile number inside my pocket alongside my GPS. It was obvious they found it weird that I didn't have a phone with me, but I threw them some half-baked reason about not wanting to risk breaking it when I go out running. At least I have some contact details of a 'safe' person in the UK if I really need it in the future.

It will be awkward giving him a hug across the controls in the middle of the car, so I decide I won't unless he initiates. Stifling a yawn, Henry waves at me as I step out of the car. It seems I won't need to worry about hugging after all.

"Take care, and thanks again," I say, giving him a smile and walk (with a forced limp) across the street in the direction of the shopping centre. Dead leaves spin and bounce along the walkway. The wind is high, increasing the night's chill factor. I hug my arms around my body and wait until he pulls away before heading east.

I don't need to use the GPS. I've memorised my route. It's simple enough – I'm heading along a straight road called Hedon Road with very few detours. It's a long road which takes me most of the way I need to go. It'll be close to midnight by the time I get there, but I'll still have a good few hours before my ship departs. There are swathes of industrial land on either side of the road and some stretches with houses on either side. The hour passes quickly. To keep my blood pumping and the cold at bay, I stride along at a pace. Because it's a main road and there's a continuous trickle of traffic even at this time of night, I feel safe enough. I'm less likely to be jumped at, anyway.

The creaking and clanging of cranes lifting containers alerts me that I've hit my destination. It's just east of the commercial port which heads out to places like Rotterdam. At first, I stand well back near the road and observe the layout of the freight port. It's roughly the size of an airport terminal, and there are a few vehicles dotted about in the open space closest to where I'm standing. I crouch down behind a 4x4 and peep out. Dispersed around the port, there're a few men in overalls looking purposeful and two freight ships docked up at the quays. What I need to do is get a bit closer to the low corrugated metal building, which appears to be an office. There will hopefully be more information there regarding quays and timetables. In front of the building, there are rows upon rows of large rectangular containers. Even though it's dark, I can see from the spotlights that the container bodies display a good spectrum of colours.

I glance at my watch and it's just past midnight. It's over four hours till my ship departs, but I wanted to get here early enough to figure out the lay of the land. Any later, and I'd have been hanging around longer than was necessary in the city centre.

In one sense, being seen is not that big a deal, I guess. I could always cry ignorance and claim I got lost trying to find the commercial port. My main concern is with the wrong type of people.

An overweight man in overalls lumbers out of the office door heading to my right. He's puffing on what looks like a vaporizer. Squinting, I notice that his skin is dark and most likely East Asian. With a racing heart, I duck out of my hiding place and walk as nonchalantly as I can towards the man.

He glances at me, and I throw out a few words hoping they'll catch the right fish. "I'm trying to find a man called Sabu. I don't suppose you know where he is?"

He stops walking and looks me up and down. "Sabu? Yes, I'm Sabu. Just hold on one moment and I'll be with you shortly." He is so serious, then I realise that he has one of those faces with a naturally down-turned mouth. Turning his back to me slightly, he fumbles in the pocket of his overalls for something.

While I stand to one side of him, waiting, it's like a fridge door opens and light flicks on in my brain. *He's lying.*

As quickly as the thought landed, I turn on my heels and run to my left as far away from him as I can. "Wait!" he calls out after me. "Come back!" His voice is closer than it was before. His feet are pounding the ground behind me. "You asked for my help, no?"

I'm grateful for all my running experience. He's a heavy man and not half as nimble on his feet as I am. I weave my way to the right, then the left, down one row of containers and then to the right again past another stack. I'm vaguely aiming for the eastern edge of the container park, but my main intention is just to lose him. It's not long before the noise of his panting has gone, but fear has imprinted the sound on my mind, so I can't shake the impression he's following me for longer than he does.

Buzzing with adrenalin, I press up against the end row of containers and allow my own breathing to subside.

Because of my interaction with the false 'Sabu', I missed out on seeing the information boards outside the office regarding the times of departure and location of the ships. There must be another way. I stand quietly for another ten minutes or so, then I slip down the aisle in the direction of the quay. As I approach the quay, I notice that there's large display board overhead hanging down from a metal frame. Edging around the stack of containers nearest the quay, I step even closer, glancing from side to side and trying to avoid being seen. I'm too close to the ships now to convincingly pretend that I'm lost.

In clear view, the display board shows the names of the destinations, the time of departure, final loading time and the number of the bay. I scan the details and see my intended ship to Trivandrum. The final loading time is 02:30, a good two hours before departure and the bay is number four. I've still got plenty of time. The bay numbers are clearly marked on the ground in blue lighting, and bay four is currently empty. Inwardly, I pray for direction again while weaving my way around the stacked containers, searching for clues as to what I should do next. I'm not entirely sure what I'm looking for, and the precariousness of my situation hits me like a car colliding with an HGV.

Out of the corner of my eye, I see a sudden movement. A man steps out from behind one row of containers on my right and beckons at me – it's a South Indian gesture – palm and fingers pointing downwards and if I hadn't known that I might have thought it was a rude gesture. I freeze, uncertain what to do, my body pressed back against one of the containers. Next, he comes a step closer so I can see him better and presses the tips of his thumbs and forefingers together into a fishlike shape. A shiver of relief floods my veins. It's the gesture that Judy told me about! The fish symbol that the early Christians used to identify themselves in secret.

I walk towards the man, still shaking.

"You must be Sabu?" I whisper as I approach him. He's much slimmer than the pretender, and although he's not smiling, his face shines with an inner joy.

"Yes, daughter," he says in a low voice. "I noticed you running from place to place, and figured you were looking for a safe place to hide. We'll have to be quick. Are you going to India?"

"I am," I reply.

"Good, good. Follow me and don't say another word – not yet anyway."

I follow Sabu to my right as he marches to the end of the row. A voice comes through on a walkie talkie he's carrying. I don't hear what it says exactly, but Sabu replies, "I'll be five minutes."

There's a pile of containers stacked in one corner labelled

with a sign that says Kochi. Sabu takes a quick look around him then takes a wrench like tool to the back of one of the containers and opens in.

"Get inside," he whispers. "I'll come and get you out as soon as it's safe to do so."

My face must be showing some of the uncertainty I feel, because he puts one hand on my arm and says, "Don't worry. It won't be for more than a few hours."

I peer at the piles of cardboard boxes pressed up against the corrugated walls, and clamber inside and sit down against one wall near the door. I give him a questioning expression and he grins for the first time and gives me two thumbs up.

The next minute the door has closed on me and I'm hidden in a cramped, dark space once again, my heart hammering out a prayer of gratitude.

Chapter 23

In the pitch black, the light on my watch glows automatically and I can see the time is 00:32. I've got at least four hours inside this metallic hulk before the ship sets sail. It's possible Sabu may come to release me sooner, but I doubt it. I'm sure he'll have other jobs to do.

Stretching my legs out, I try to get as comfortable as I can in the space between the wall of boxes and the door. At least I've not got smelly, damp clothes on my face like I had in the last tight space I was in!

The hardest thing is going to be holding my bladder in for four hours. I've not emptied it since leaving Annie and Henry's and normally I'd be going at least every three hours. Really, I need to go... like... now!

But best not to think about it. It'll just make it worse.

Time always crawls when you're waiting for something to happen, and now is no exception. It reminds me of how much I used to fritter time away scrolling through social media feeds to stave off boredom or avoid other more pressing tasks. And I was not unusual in doing so.

Well, I can't do any of that now or for two more weeks at least... I heave a sigh.

God knows how much we need to have some things stripped away from us before we stand naked and quivering, with just ourselves and our endless thoughts, in recognition of life's small mercies.

I must have been in the container for a good forty minutes or so, before the ground under my feet begins to move. There's a straining, creaking sound as the crane – presumably – lifts the container up and my heart feels like it's plummeting in my chest – much like the sensation you get on a rollercoaster. I thrust one arm behind the box nearest me to avoid being thrown forward against the wall, and my armpit muscles ache as I grip on as tight as I can. I rock back and forth for what seems like several minutes, but in reality must be less time.

Eventually, I can feel the container being lowered and my insides settle down. There's a sweesh, sweesh sound. I imagine the container is being tied down by straps of some sort. A variety of male voices in different English accents call out from one side and another. "Tighten that strap there," "Watch out – you nearly hit your head!" and "Container number ZY18 is off balance. It's weighted to the port side..."

I curl up in a tight ball. Even though I can't be seen, in my head there's always the risk. When I was little, I remember a time there were workmen in our house, and when I went for a number two, I pushed my fingers against my ears to block out the sound. Somehow, I imagined that if I couldn't hear myself, they couldn't hear me either! It gave me a psychological privacy when surrounded by strangers who were closer than was comfortable. It's a similar feeling now.

Every nerve ending remains on full alert while the containers are being stacked and crew are toing and froing all around me.

It takes another twenty-five minutes until the sound of the last voice disappears.

Drip, drip, drip. All my attention homes in on the distinctive sound. It sounds like it's coming from somewhere nearby – no more than a few metres away from my container. What could it be? A fuel leak? Rainfall? Or something else entirely?

Suddenly, I become aware of a faint scratching and rustling inside the container. Every hair follicle stands on end. A mouse – or worse – is in here – with me. The fact that I can see nothing makes it even more skin-crawling. I don't like rodents at the best of times and living in an old house most of my life, I've encountered a few. This is far worse than being in a tight space. I wouldn't call myself mousophobic (or whatever you call it!), but I'm borderline. Anything small, hairy and scuttling sets my teeth on edge. It sounds to me like it's chewing away on the edge of something a few metres away from me. It's not likely to be at all interested in me, but... Eeugh, it's getting closer.

Not only that, but my bladder is ballooning in my abdomen, and I am fearful that if something out of the ordinary happens – I won't be able to hold on much longer. If only I'd taken a quick pee somewhere along Hedon Road rather than waiting... But it's not that easy if you're a girl, is it?

I wish I could sing or something. It would focus my mind on something else. Obviously, I can't as it would draw attention to me, but then it strikes me that I may not be able to sing aloud, but I can sing in my head – so to speak. I have to concentrate really hard in order to spool some songs out of my memory and ironically the first ones that come to my mind are inane pop songs with a simple, repetitive beat. I want to laugh but have to contain that too, and the nearing scratching of my rodent companion sends a wave of nausea over me as I fight competing emotions.

I take a deep breath. *Come on Sathya. I might be a screw of contradictions right now, but God is still with me.* The words of Psalm 23 imprint themselves in my mind. It's also the lines of a contemporary worship song so I'm both 'singing' and speaking truth over myself at the same time. "Even though I walk through the darkest valley, I will fear no evil; for you are with me; your rod and your staff, they comfort me..." In the song, the lines "For you are with me," are repeated three times in a rap like rhythm and as I sing them, the nausea vanishes, and my heartbeat slows.

My mouse companion suddenly doesn't seem quite so revolting. Poor thing – it's simply trying to survive, just like the rest of us are.

That being said... *please don't crawl on me, please*! Almost without realising it, I've said the words aloud. At the sound of my whisper the scratching stops for a moment and I hear the animal scurrying away from me.

I repeat the worship song over and over a few times, and I'm almost starting to enjoy myself when, at last – there's a fumbling at the door and a faint creaking of metal against metal as the container opens.

"Quick, daughter, take my hand," Sabu mutters as soon as his face appears around the opening doors. It's only dim lighting outside, but I've been in blackness for long enough that my eyes squint against the contrasting brightness. "There'll be time for explanations soon enough."

I can see soon enough why he's asked me to take his hand. My container is on the second row of stacks, so I can't just simply step out. It also hits me that Sabu knew exactly which container to place me in. If I'd been put in the middle of a row of containers, I'd not have been able to get out easily.

"The crew are all in the briefing room right now, so you have nothing to fear."

I crouch forward to the edge of the container, lowering my legs over the side. There's a frame like structure on either side of the container. I put one foot against the side of the frame about halfway down, one hand against the side and hold out my other hand to Sabu. He takes my weight as I jump, landing with a bounce on the balls of my feet to avoid jarring my back.

"Thank you," I say, my mouth dry. The jump has increased my urgency to pee. "I hope there's somewhere I can go to the toilet soon?"

"No problem," Sabu says. "Follow me."

I follow his reassuring shape along the edges of the vast Lego-like bulk of the container bay, with containers packed floor to ceiling. The ship's side is on my right hand but it's not very high and above is nothing but space and a few lights twinkling. I gaze above me at the British night sky for what might be my last chance in a long time.

Within a minute or two we've reached the superstructure – the tall accommodation block for the crew. Despite Sabu telling me that I've nothing to fear, my pulse throbs in my ears as I step over the edge of the entrance into the building, knowing that if I were to get caught now, not only would it be the end for me, but it would signal the loss of Sabu's livelihood.

Sabu takes me down a flight of metal stairs to the lower ground floor. The corridor stretching away a few metres in the distance is narrow, dimly lit and gloomy. As we walk down it, I can see that most of the doors are not labelled. Pausing in his walk, Sabu glances around him and presses his finger against a door sensor on our right. The door is marked with a small sign indicating that this is a store cupboard. The door swings open and we step inside a space that is around 1.5 metre wide by 3 metres long, barely big enough to swing a cat in, as Dad likes to say. There are cupboards along both sides of the room and a mattress in the furthest corner with a duvet and pillow neatly folded on top.

I don't have time to take everything in before Sabu turns to me and says, "Here near the door is a bucket with a lid that you can use for your toilet needs – I will take it away for cleaning every day. It won't be safe to use the ship's toilet apart from occasionally. You can use it now – like I said all the crew are in the briefing room four floors above this one – but for your own safety you'll need to stick with this bucket for most of the time. I know it's not ideal."

He wobbles his head from side to side and smiles at me. "I won't hold you any longer. The toilet is just opposite this room. Go now then come straight back."

A few minutes later, I'm back in the storeroom with Sabu. He's picked up a steam mop and bucket and holds them in his hands while he talks.

"So, this is going to be your home for the next two weeks. It's not very luxurious I'm afraid, but it's the best I can do. You'll be the fourth person who's used this space since I started helping people escape about six months ago. I'm presuming you're a believer given you knew about me?" he asks.

I nod vigorously.

"Praise the Lord," he continues. "We do what we can to support our brothers and sisters in need. First things first: I'll enable your fingerprint on the sensor device into this room so that you can get in and out easily without compromising your security. Secondly, I'll bring you some food if you need any?"

"Not right now," I say. "Just something to drink would be nice. As soon as I can, I think I'll sleep." I want to ask him all sorts of questions, but as the adrenalin gradually subsides, a numbing exhaustion has hit me.

"Good, good," he says, taking out a bottle of water from one of the cupboards and handing it to me. "We'll just get your fingerprint set up then I'll leave you be..."

Chapter 24

Mum, Dad and Naomi loom over me like Titans. I'm sitting on the floor straining my neck up at them. Their faces have that slightly distorted demeanour that comes from looking up at a height. All three of them are frowning and yelling at me.

"Look at you now – you're trapped!" Mum screeches.

"You thought God would save you, but he didn't!" Naomi yells.

Even mild-mannered Dad is shouting – "You've got to meet us halfway. There's only so much we can do!"

"Stop shouting at me, stop shouting at me!" I cry, curling up into a ball so that I can't see their faces anymore.

I begin humming to myself to block out the sound of their rebukes. Then suddenly, there's the rumble of an earthquake beneath me and my body shakes. My family's voices fade, and I wake up in the dimness of the storeroom, the vibration of the ship's engine mirroring the rumbling of the earth in my dream – or should I say nightmare?

I unfurl my body from the slightly awkward position that I've been sleeping in and lie flat on my back. It's 10:46. Even though I've slept well, there's a shaky, sickening feeling snaking through me.

What am I doing here – stuck in the belly of a container ship? Wouldn't I have just been better off submitting to the tolerance agenda? Then I'd still be home right now, smugly content and preparing to go to the university of my dreams. Instead, here I am, everything that I know and everyone that I love having slithered off me like Hamlet's mortal coil. Was it really worth it?

Sighing, I fling off the duvet, and get up to use the toilet bucket. There's one of those tiny sinks near the back of the room so I can wash my hands without any problems.

Near the door on the floor is one of those cardboard containers like you get on a plane. I pick it up and peel the lid off. Sabu must have left it for me earlier, rather than wake me up. Inside is a bread roll with a tiny sliver of butter in a packet and a decent sized omelette. There's also a small cup of orange juice, just big enough to fit inside the container and stainless-steel cutlery. Perched on the edge of my bed, I gobble up my breakfast gratefully. I expect the omelette to be limp and cold, but it's warm and comforting.

As there's no window inside the room, there's no natural lighting to give away the time of day. I'm thankful for my working watch, which gives me some measure of time, at least.

How am I going to fill my time? The two weeks travel time ahead of me yawns like an empty chasm. I have nothing to do other than sleep, eat, think and pray. Too much time to think is never a good thing; it's when all the negative thoughts and ideas set up camp in your mind. Or maybe it's just me? I've never had this much time to do nothing before and it scares me.

I stand up and begin doing some star jumps. As soon as the floor begins creaking under my weight, I realise that this might not be such a good idea after all and stop. An instant giveaway of my presence if nothing else. There's not much chance of me getting exercise then while I'm stuck inside. At best, I can walk up and down this tiny space, unless I can figure out an agreement with Sabu for getting out on the deck occasionally.

The worst thing are the thoughts churning through my mind. The words of Naomi in my nightmare are torturing me. *You thought God would save you, but he didn't!* My head is grinding with the agony of wanting to deny this, but the words keep kicking my brain until I start to wonder – maybe she's right? Have I just wasted my whole life, hopes and dreams for a god that either doesn't exist or is cruel?

I want to pray, but I feel like I'm in a decompression chamber after being underwater for a long time. My ears are popping, and my chest is tight. I'm alive, but I can't concentrate on anything other than the here and now.

I lie down on my bed again and hum to myself and keep humming until a modicum of peace fills me.

I must have been lying here for a while humming when there is a gentle beeping at the door and Sabu pokes his head around the door to check whether I'm awake or not. I don't want him to leave again, so I force myself to rise. I prop my head up on my arm and plaster a smile on my face. I don't want to look like death to him. After all, he did save my life.

Sabu comes in and sits cross legged on the floor at a respectful distance.

"Good morning, daughter. You ate something?"

Of course, this is always the respectful first question in South India – not whether you slept well but whether you ate well.

"Yes, I did, thank you. My name is Sathya, by the way."

"Sathya, Sathya. A beautiful name so full of meaning. Your

mother or father is Indian, no?"

"Yes, my mum is. She's actually from Kerala."

"Good, good – God's own country," he says, a grin cracking his weather-beaten face.

"They say that about Yorkshire, where I'm from too," I say.

"I can't spend long now, as I've got to cook lunch soon, but I just wanted to check if there's anything you need: clothes, books etc? I would give you a phone, but I don't have a spare one I can give you I'm afraid. Though if there's anything that you need to check, let me know and I can lend you mine."

"If you have any spare clothes, that would be amazing... Do you have a Bible I could borrow? Or anything else that I can read or do?"

Sabu purses his lips then says, "My daughter is about the same size as you. I have a few of her items I can lend you. She handed me a bag before I left and said to me, 'Just in case you meet a young woman like me, Dad.'" He beams. "God knew you were coming! He cares about the little details, no?" He pauses, waiting for a reaction from me.

I nod and that seems to be enough for him.

"You can definitely have a Bible. I have one in English – unless you read Malayalam?"

"I don't, no. I speak it a little but have never learnt to read."

"I will see if I can find anything else to keep you occupied. Boredom will be your main problem here, no?"

He stands up, not waiting for my reply. "I must go. I'll be back with your lunch shortly."

The door closes behind him and I stand up, inhaling and exhaling deeply. His companionship and his faith have lifted my spirits a little. All the same, I'm going to struggle in this space for two weeks. I need to be real with myself about that.

Although I'm safer in this hull than I've been for several months now, that's part of the problem. The lack of fear, the lack of momentum and the lack of adrenalin are crushing me, putting me in a darker place than I've felt in a long time. I entered the ship in the early hours of the 16th February, and I've been here three days so far. We will arrive in India on the 2nd March, and I'm counting down every sluggish, dragging day.

Despite Sabu faithfully bringing me everything that he promised, including a small pile of girl's clothes, a hairbrush, a toothbrush and toothpaste, a well-thumbed Bible and a randomly selected pile of magazines and puzzle books that he'd gathered from somewhere, I still haven't picked up the Bible.

I can't explain it to myself, let alone to anyone else, but it's like I want to punish myself or – dare I say it? – punish God himself for putting me in this position in the first place. I am wallowing in this dark place. I won't say I'm enjoying it, that would be too weird, but I'm rolling in the slime, allowing it to slosh over me, drown me.

It's not all about me and my pain either – after all one part of me is so grateful that I'm on my way to safety – but I keep visualising the faces of Bahman, Kate and Maggie and guilt crawls over me. As far as I know they're still in that horrible place. Why me? What makes me so special that I should be free? Will they get out before they're so crushed in their spirits that they can never recover? I know that sounds hopeless, but that's the way I feel right now.

I'll be honest with you – I've been crying a lot. This morning when Sabu came to bring me breakfast, I had been crying since waking up and I'm sure Sabu could see it all over my face. He said nothing other than, "I'll keep praying for you, daughter,"

182

and reached out a hand to rub my shoulder.

I'm glad. I didn't want him to say anything more. I didn't want him to pry and get me to bare my trembling soul. I'm just happy for him to acknowledge my pain and be done with it.

Just before lunch, I lay down the Sudoku puzzle I've been dipping into, curl up again on my bed and toy with the edge of the duvet. There is a hollow in my core like I'm being sucked into a deep, deep pit with no way out. As I lie there, I become aware of the creeping sensation of tiny bugs crawling all over my skin. It can't be real, it can't be! But no matter how hard I try to rationalise, the feeling continues. I jump up out of my bed and explode: *Get off me now!* For a moment, I'm terrified I said the words aloud, but I've become so conditioned to keeping quiet that I'm relieved when I realise that the words were screamed in my head. Only. Just.

What's the matter with me? Am I going through some sort of psychosis or what?

In that electric, fearful moment a quiet voice probes my spirit – *Philippians. Read the book of Philippians.*

I will do, Lord, I sob, snot running down my lips. *Forgive me for pushing you away.*

I'm trembling as I pick up the unread Bible from the cupboard shelf where I've left it. I won't forget the time about two years ago when Mayeso was teaching us youngsters about the book of Philippians being the 'joy book'. Unlike happiness, he reminded us that joy is not an emotion based on our circumstances. Spiritual joy is deeper, wider and supernatural. Am I ready to access joy again or do I want to continue in this cloudy coil? The answer waits eagerly for me even as I thumb my way through the Bible to find the book. My heart pounds with expectation.

Sitting on the edge of the bed, I read all four chapters through once and then twice. I fill my mind with its truth.

"I will continue to rejoice, for I know that through your prayers and God's provision of the Spirit of Jesus Christ what has happened to me will turn out for my deliverance." The notes in the Bible's margins remind me that at the time the Apostle Paul wrote these words he was in prison. Suffering was very much a lived experience for him.

"I know what it is to be in need, and I know what it is to have plenty. I have learned the secret of being content in any and every situation, whether well fed or hungry, whether living in plenty or in want. I can do all this through him who gives me strength."

I finish reading it and sigh with relief. God has been with me through all of this. If I start counting the ways in which God has helped me, I'd be on my knees in awe. As Sabu said, it's in the little details: Marie's word for me about the GPS; the friendship of Kate and Maggie in the Matrix centre; Bahman helping me get out; meeting Judy and her insight regarding Sabu; Annie and Henry feeding me and loving me; and, of course, meeting Sabu himself. Every little detail stacking up to the miracle that is my life's story. (As for my friends in the centre, I need to trust God for them – I shouldn't have to bear the guilt for something I've not done).

Tears run down my cheeks again, but this time my spirit is lighter.

Chapter 25

I lick garlicky oil off my fingers and push the empty food container away. Masala dosa, samba and coconut chutney – my favourite.

"Mmm," I murmur contentedly, wiping my face and hands.

"You liked it?" Sabu asks. It's one of the few times when he's stayed around to talk while I eat my lunch. His companionship has been one of the things that has warmed my heart throughout my time on this ship.

"Absolutely," I say, giving him a grin. "You must make your wife very happy," I say, then blush, as that of course could have a double meaning.

"Ah, she is a super cook," he says, oblivious to my Freudian slip.

"I've been wondering – how did you get into this whole business of rescuing people like myself?"

Sabu shifts his position. "Good question. It was a chance encounter that opened my eyes to what was going on in Europe and the UK. About a year ago, I was traveling like this by freight between Hull and Kochi when one of the other staff – a Muslim man from France – told me that this was his last job on board as he'd been laid off. I asked him why, and he told me he'd expressed some views that weren't very popular. I felt so sad about this kindly man losing his job simply for expressing an opinion that I started doing some research, and I rapidly learnt all about the so-called tolerance agenda.

"At the same time, I'd been learning about Harriet Tubman and her role in bringing enslaved black Americans from the southern states of America into safety in Canada, and I felt a stirring in my spirit. I can't compare myself to her – the mighty warrior that she was – but I knew God was calling me to do what I could to help in however small a way. I knew that I had to start somewhere so I did. I simply pray and ask God to help me find those who look to be on the run. And it happens from there."

"I was told about you from a lady I met while on the run. She'd heard about you from some contacts in her church. How does that work? How do you get the word out? I'd not heard anything from my church."

"It's been a word-of-mouth thing so far. Perhaps your friend's church is one of the one's that I've had connections with because of those that I've helped so far? I don't want to spread the word too widely as I don't want to put people in danger, so I've had to be very careful whom to share my offer of help with and who not to. I'm treading very cautiously here. You know Jesus asked his followers to be as wise as serpents as well as innocent as doves... I need to remind myself that it's not about me and my good name, but about you precious souls. God clearly wanted you to find me, so he placed this lady into your path."

I nod thoughtfully. It's now five days into our trip and I'm wondering whether it's too much for me to ask. "I don't want to put either of us into danger, but do you think there's any safe way of me being able to get out on deck occasionally get a bit of fresh air and exercise? Don't worry if not, but I just wanted to ask." I bite my lip anxiously. I don't want to cause him any trouble.

Lifting his head, Sabu makes eye contact with me. "I'll have a think about it and get back to you. I'd better get on with my work now. I'll be back with your dinner later."

Six hours later, Sabu enters the room, hands me my dinner and stands shifting from side to side near the door. It's a sign that he's not going to be coming in for a long chat.

"At 3am – there's just the one helmsman at work. Everyone else is off duty at that time and should be asleep. He will be in the commanding station. In theory, he has access via CCTV to all parts of the ship, but if you head back along the deck to the container area and stay at the stern, he won't notice you as he'll be focussed on steering the ship safely and that's it."

He hands me a piece of paper with a diagram of the parts of the ship sketched on it, "No more than half an hour and not every night please and there should be no problem."

"Thank you," I say. "I really appreciate your thought and care."

At 3am, my alarm wakes me up. Yawning, I get out of bed and shove my feet into my trainers, squashing down the tops of the heels. Naomi would tell me off for putting my shoes on that way. She is always meticulous at undoing her shoes before putting her feet in. Although bleary eyed, I'm soon buzzing with excitement. Stealthily, I open the door and head back slowly and quietly along the corridor, up the stairs, and to the deck. As soon as I hit the deck, the fresh air hits me and I gasp with delight.

A memory washes over me – Naomi and I camping in the back-garden in the middle of August when we were ten years old. I'd woken up to go to the toilet, leaving Naomi sleeping on her side, with her arm twisted back around her body in that endearing way she had. I'd rushed into the house to use the downstairs toilet then walked back into the garden flashing my torch around. Realising I didn't need it, I switched off my torch. The sky was so unusually bright with stars that I'd stood there for a moment, flung my head back and gazed in wide eyed wonder. I'd been so excited by the beauty of creation that I'd woken up Naomi and started chattering to her then and there. She wasn't too impressed at being woken – I can tell you now!

Making my way down the ship now, I smile wryly to myself at the memory. What I wouldn't give now to have the opportunity to wake my sister up and tell her about my experiences. Sadness scrapes down my throat.

I savour the sensation of my leg muscles working again and the air blowing around the nape of my neck. It's not cold. I don't know exactly where we are, but I'd imagine we're closer to the equator now.

It's several hundred metres to walk from the superstructure to the stern of the ship and I keep up a brisk pace. Despite Sabu telling me I can spend half an hour outside, I don't intend to spend more time than it takes to walk to the stern and then back again. Even that will be enough to shake away the cobwebs and make me feel fully alive again. If I do this every three nights or so, it will help me get through this time more easily.

At the stern, I crane my head out over the edge of the ship and look out into the dark distance. I can see little other than deep blue backwash lit by the taillights of the ship and the shadowy outline of a coast on the port side. Squinting against the sea-spray, I try to imagine where the coastline could be, but it could be anywhere, so I quickly give up. I'm pretty ignorant as far as sea routes from the UK to India are concerned. That reminds me – I need to ask Sabu. He can give me a better idea.

The next day, Sabu takes out his phone and shows me the route in all its 3D splendid colour. It's fascinating. From Hull you follow the North Sea down to the Atlantic Ocean and all the way round to the southern tip of Spain through to the Mediterranean Sea. Then at the north-eastern tip of the Med, you hit the Suez Canal and head south through the Red Sea till you hit the Gulf of Aden south of Yemen and out into the Indian Ocean.

"Right now, we're around here," he says, pointing to the Mediterranean Sea north of Libya. "It's probably the coast of Crete or one of the other Greek islands that you saw last night if you were looking port side. We didn't get close enough to the Libyan coast for you to see it."

"So much to know and understand!" I say, widening my eyes.

"And so much time left to explore," Sabu says with a twinkle, allowing the holographic map to flicker off. "You're so young. God willing, you've got the rest of your life to explore all the wonders of this world."

At his words, a thrill runs through me. He's right. The adventures ahead are boundless and undiscovered. Momentarily, the fact of not getting into university, losing my statehood and being separated from my family fade in significance.

Chapter 26

I t's the final day of February. In just two days we'll be docking in India, and the atmosphere is becoming warmer and more humid the closer we get. I'm grateful for the lighter, more summery clothes that Sabu's daughter has passed on and I've taken to walking around bare foot to keep cool. Despite its thermo-adaptable material, that horrible, institutional onesie would have left me sweating if I'd had to wear it all the time.

Time has passed slowly, and I won't pretend that I've not slid into fear or depression again, but I'm refusing to stay in that dark place and have done everything that I can to keep the fire of hope stoked.

Every three days I've headed outside to the deck. Despite it being the middle of the night, I won't pretend I've not been anxious of getting caught, but thankfully there's been no sign of life, other than the odd rat or mice scurrying around. Being outside occasionally has boosted me, given me energy and increased my mental capacity.

Given the dearth of reading material, I've pretty much read through the whole Bible. I'm trying to approach it in a devo-tional, prayerful way, but at the same time I've been spending three to four hours a day reading it, which has inevitably led to large chunks being read in one go. Every magazine that Sabu has brought me, I've devoured – regardless of whether I'm interested in the subject matter or not – and he's bought me a few random ones like motorcycle mechanics!

I've also been ploughing my way through the puzzle books he's given me, including logic problems, Sudoku and crosswords. Not long ago, Dad told me that puzzles like these are losing their interest as a leisure activity, but I'm sold. Maybe it's because there's been little else to do, but I love the way they engage your brain. It beats scrolling mindlessly through the fascinating but never-ending whirlpool of information and ideas on the internet, where you constantly feel like you're never engaged enough and always missing out on something just around the corner. I'm definitely going to have to get more disciplined about my screen time once I'm back online.

I've also been dabbling in poetry writing. I started scribbling a few lines on the back pages of the puzzle book and, when Sabu saw me doing that one day, he provided me with some lined paper. "Leaves mulching / Tears falling / Bodies colliding – / In expansive space and time / I wander, muse and drive forward..." I can't pretend any of it is brilliant poetry, but it's helping me express my thoughts and feelings and I'm enjoying the discipline of doing so in a succinct, tight way.

Inevitably, I've had lots of time to sleep, and I'm well rested and impatient to get out onto dry land again. The question is what am I going to do and how am I going to get out safely? I've put off thinking about it, but as the time draws nearer, I realise I can't put it off any longer. It requires another conversation with Sabu.

"Have you got time to sit and talk?" I say, glancing up at Sabu as he brings in the usual lunch container. This time it's a north Indian dish – naan bread and a tomatoey paneer curry. If you've never tried paneer, I'd encourage you to – it's a deliciously light and smooth cheese, closer to mozzarella than feta, which I've never got into.

"Sure, sure. Ten minutes at least," he says, sitting cross legged on the floor at his usual respectful distance.

I've already told him about my Indian family so he's aware of them, but one thing we've not discussed is the logistics of getting from the Cochin docks to their village home nor how I'm going to claim asylum. I have no idea how the asylum system works in India.

He looks at me. "You want to know how you're going to get off this ship, no?"

I nod and smile. "Yes, that's one thing." Don't tell me that men are not intuitive. Sabu is one of the most intuitive, sensitive people I've ever met.

"Ok, ok. So, a couple of hours before we land in Kochi, I will get you back in the same container as you entered the ship."

"Remind me what time we arrive?" I interject as politely as I can.

"09:33. I'll give you a bread roll or something else light to eat beforehand. I wouldn't take breakfast onto the container with you as it's too dark for you to see properly and you might spill food. After everything is unloaded and the crew have left for the day, only then will I get you out. I have a man on the ground – an auto driver – who can take you to your destination. Don't go with anyone but him. I'll introduce you to him as soon as it's safe to do so. What else do you want to know?" He rapidly strokes his calf muscle with one thumb. If I didn't know him better, I'd have thought that was a gesture of impatience.

"How do I go about claiming asylum?" Once again, the hard reality of my situation hits me, and I feel like I've been punched in the stomach.

"There's no shame in being a refugee, daughter. Our Lord himself was one in Egypt as a small child."

"Yes," I say quietly, "But still. I never expected..."

"Nobody ever expects to be in that situation," Sabu says gently. "It's just painful to you because you thought of the UK as being a safe, democratic, free place – until recently. And why shouldn't you?

"So, in terms of asylum – there are only two places in India that currently process asylum claims – Delhi and Chennai – although I'm sure this is going to change soon. It's done at the UNHCR offices and you have to do it in person. You can't just apply online. What I suggest you do is simply go and spend some time with your family first – and only then go to claim asylum at a time when one of your family can support you with the process. It's crucial," (here Sabu pinches his thumb together with his forefinger and middle finger for emphasis) "that you don't try to do it alone. Community support is so very important in an Indian context, as I'm sure you know."

"Got it," I say. Nerves flutter up and down my stomach and I find myself surprisingly tongue tied.

I haven't picked up my food yet, as I've been too engrossed, but now I tear off a piece of naan and scoop some curry up with it. I'm not hungry but am itching to do something with my hands.

The food moves slowly down my throat, as if crawling over sticky boulders. I become conscious of being exposed and vulnerable. I've gone all this way on my own: standing up for what I believe, being captured and running away, and I should be feeling fierce and bold, but here I am – a girl simply wanting reassurance and love.

A few tears trickle down my cheeks, and in that moment, Sabu gives me just what I need. "Come, come, daughter," he says, enveloping my slouching figure in a hug. I return the hug, my shoulders shaking as I sob uncontrollably.

On the morning of the 2nd March, I wake well before my alarm. I'd set it for 6:45 am to give me time for last minute packing and a quick wash, but it's just gone 6am. I'm buzzing and can't lie down any longer.

After brushing my teeth and taking a wash at the sink, I put on a pair of jeans and a dark green churidar. I throw all the other clothes in the backpack that Sabu has provided for me along with my poems and the puzzle books. With a grimace, I leave the onesies in the bin bag that Sabu left me. I'm sorry, but would you want to keep an item of clothing that came out of a place of oppression? I certainly don't. The only things I'll keep are the trainers. I have little choice as they're the only footwear I've got.

This time, I'll make sure I go for a pee before getting inside the container. I hope Sabu will let me go to the proper toilet this time rather than using the bucket. By 6:20, I have everything organised, so I take the time before Sabu arrives to steady my mind and spirit. I will leave Sabu's Bible for him in case it's needed by anyone else, but I take a few minutes to read through the jars of clay passage that encouraged me so much after finding out about Naomi's betrayal all those months ago. After reading the passage in 2 Corinthians, I pray.

Be with me, Lord. Sustain me, mould me, guide me. Be my sword, my shield and my strength. Help me to find Namita Aunty and family and I pray that they will be welcoming and understanding. Guide me as I make contact with my parents and Naomi again, and help me to communicate with wisdom and love. You know the path ahead and I don't, so help me to trust in you whatever the outcome. Thank you, Lord. In Jesus' name. Amen.

I stand up and pace around this tiny space that has been my home for the past two weeks. It's been hard being cooped up, but I'm so grateful for the protection that it's given me, and I kiss my fingers and press them to the walls. *Let this place be a blessing to whoever uses it after me.*

I keep checking my watch impatiently. It's 6:43 when Sabu knocks at the door. I presume he didn't just walk in on the off chance I was getting dressed. "Come in," I say as quietly as I can. He enters the room. A huge smile cracks his weather-beaten face.

"It's the first day of your new life," he tells me, then hands me a bread roll filled with curried tuna and a piece of paper. "These are my contact details, daughter. Keep them with you and do tell me how you get on."

I fold up the paper tightly and shove it into my jeans pocket. "Thank you for all you've done for me, Uncle. I'll never forget you." I give him a hug now as I don't know when I'll next get the chance.

"Oh, my dear, may God bless you with this next stage of your life. I'll tell Anu all about you and maybe one day you'll have the chance to meet her. Please, do eat up your roll, then you can use the ship's toilet before I take you to the container. The staff are in the briefing room for twenty minutes or so."

"I'm not hungry," I say.

"Eat," Sabu urges with a sideways head tilt, so I munch away at my breakfast and finish within two minutes.

I'm sweating inside the container. Despite how early it is, it must be almost 30 degrees Celsius outside, and inside is even hotter. I keep taking sips from the water bottle Sabu has given me to stay hydrated. I don't want to guzzle it down too quickly as it could be a long time before I get another drink.

When the ship's engine turned off around twenty minutes ago, it took me a few seconds to figure out what was different. The continuous, gentle vibration I'd got used to after two weeks at sea had stopped.

Now, I breathe shallow breaths while workers mill around my container and the familiar sound of creaking and clanging fills my head space. With all the surrounding commotion, it's unlikely anyone can hear me, but I don't want to risk it. My heart pounds and I'm a little light-headed. At this final stage of my escape, somehow what's at stake feels taut and twangy like guy ropes after the rain. The strange sensation that I can be seen through the metal walls is strong and real in my mind, even though logic tells me it's impossible. What's logical, anyway? How much of what has happened in the past month has made any sense whatsoever, let alone fit the so-called rules of logic?

An overwhelming desire to laugh at the craziness of it all bubbles up inside. I rapidly stuff it down. That really could be the end of me, not to mention Sabu!

Soon, I'm up in the air again with that heart plunging sensation, then lowered slowly to the accompaniment of nasal South Indian voices. Thanks to my mum's training, I can understand and speak a few basic words of Malalayam, but certainly not to any technical or academic level. I recognise the words "Slow", "careful" and "over here," but that's about it.

I'm hoping that I won't have to stay inside this airtight container much longer. My t-shirt is already drenched in sweat and sticking to my back and chest. It's nearly always hot in Kerala, but it just happens that March is the beginning of the hottest, most humid season.

I'm suddenly grateful that I've not arrived at an airport or a train station with their heaving throngs of humanity. Once the crew have left for the day, there really won't be too many people around. And, if anyone does ask questions about my presence at the port, I can always pretend to be someone's relative. Being half Indian will have its advantages. My heart rate slows.

An unknown man circulates my container talking rapidly. I hear the English words 'container' and 'dry goods' amid a load of unfamiliar Malayalam words, and my heart rate increases again. *He's not going to be opening my container up, is he? It has to be Sabu, it has to. He'll look out for me, he will. He's done so up till now.*

The sound of doors clanging alerts me that nearby containers are being opened. Then the heave, ho-ing of stored items begins. My nerves are tense, but I try to breathe slowly and stay as calm as possible. It would be absolutely no good if a stranger opened my container and I panicked.

I can hardly bear to wait much longer, before the nearby sound of workers dwindles, and I am left with nothing but the distant sound of cranes and the occasional squawk of a seagull.

Chapter 27

I 'm so relieved when my container is flung open with a clang, that I have no idea who's opened it. A wall of warm air greets me, but it's fresh salt-tinged air, far better than being cooped up in a narrow, airless space.

Whoever opened it has stood back from the door. I squint into the brightness, stand up and step out of the container.

Thankfully, it is Sabu – standing to one side grinning at me. Like the Hull port, there are rows upon rows of containers around us, but all in the glare of a blazing Indian morning.

"It's good to see that you've not been eaten alive inside the container," Sabu says, relaxed enough to joke with me.

"What would have eaten me?" I ask, playing along.

"All those tiny rats and mice, you know – fierce beasts."

Somewhat light-headed, I laugh. I wasn't even thinking about rodents this time round, thankfully. If I had, I might not have been quite so patient.

Sea breeze cools the sweaty fabric of my top against my skin.

"Come with me to the end of this row of containers. I need you to meet Jintu, your driver."

This time, I don't follow behind Sabu, but stumble beside him, my legs wobbly after being at sea for so long.

"You'll soon get used to solid ground," he says, observing the way I walk.

"I hope so," I say with a gurn, sidestepping a pile of rotting banana skins.

At the end of the rows of containers, a stocky figure is crouched next to his vehicle. It's a tiny vehicle – an autorick-shaw or 'auto' for short, looking for all the world like a metallic squashed fly. When he sees us coming, he stands up and waves us over. Behind him is a long strip of thick green grass and piles of bagged rubbish. In the hazy distance across what seems to be a bridge, lies the city of Cochin. The freight port is out on a peninsular just out from the mainland.

Jintu nods his head at me and begins talking rapidly to Sabu, assuming I can't understand, I presume. To be fair, I only pick up on a few words. "Money", "location" and "house" and I can only guess at the overall meaning. Sabu intersperses his companion's outpouring with a few affirming grunts.

"He doesn't need any money from you. It's all part of the arrangement I have with him," Sabu says to me when Jintu has finished talking, snorted loudly and moved to take his place in the driver's seat.

"Of course."

A few men and women wearing overalls and looking purpose-ful are beginning to mill around again near the auto, but no one takes any notice of me. Why would they? The realisation that no one is out to get me hits me. My head and shoulders feel lighter, like there's been an unburdening.

I smile broadly at Sabu and fling my arms out wide.

"It feels good, no?" He doesn't wait for my reply but continues. "I presume you know the village and house where your aunty lives, no? So, you must direct Jintu there. You will

199

be safe with him, no worries. He's a good man, also a believer."

A lump comes to my throat as I take in the now familiar face of the man who's become like a father to me. I lower my head and chew my lip to avoid tearing up.

Sabu puts a hand on my shoulder and rubs it. "May all go well with you, daughter. Peace be with you," he says and brings his nose close to my cheek and inhales deeply. It's a gesture that means the same as a kiss.

Deep in my spirit, I sense that this is not the end of our relationship. I don't know what the future holds yet, but he'll be a part of it – somehow.

Clutching my bag, I slide through the open side of the auto onto the spacious seat.

"God bless you, Uncle. Thank you so much!" I call as Jintu starts up the auto.

One of my earliest memories of India was coming here on a family holiday when I was five. I remember Naomi and I laughing uproariously over the judder of the auto engine that we used on a tour around Cochin. I've no idea what we found so funny. Like vehicles all over the world, autos are now electric, so you don't get that same shuddering.

As Jintu turns the auto round, I wave at Sabu, who stands and watches until we've passed over the bridge, then turns and heads back towards the port.

"Turn left at the crossroads, Uncle," I tell Jintu in Malayalam. I lean forward to make sure he has heard me. He's no more my uncle than Sabu, but we use Aunty and Uncle as a sign of respect for people who are older than us here. I learnt that long ago. You would never call someone by their first name unless they are your peer and, even then, you'd called them their name with the designation 'sister' or 'brother' attached.

Branches strung with brown nutmeg brush against me as Jintu turns the auto round the corner. The engine strains as it powers up the hill. We've reached the village in which my relatives live. I'm glad that I paid attention to where we were going whenever we came here in the past. Thankfully, I'm remembering all the relevant landmarks. All that geeky interest in places that I had when growing up has paid off.

Each brightly painted house that we pass on the way up the hill has land of at least an acre. You don't have to be loaded in Kerala in order to have a decent size property. You simply need good connections and a respectable income. This area was decimated in the horrific floods of 2018 and 2031, and after Namita Aunty's house got battered by floods twice, they decided to up sticks and build a house further up in the hills.

The roadside is smattered with coconut trees and other tropical plants as well as the type of trees that you might see in the west too. I inhale the sweet smell of frangipani flowers and smile to myself. My sensory delight is genuine, but it can't cover the knot of nervousness in my stomach.

What happens if Namita Aunty is angry with me for turning up out of the blue? They can't, they won't kick me out, surely...? How are my parents and Naomi going to react when I finally contact them after being missing for nearly three weeks? What happens if nobody's home? After all, it's Friday so most of the family will be out and about – at work and school or whatever. Unless my Ammamma is with them still...? Let's hope she's pottering around the house.

The auto continues to pull slowly up the hill until it reaches a bend in the road. My heart beats harder. I remember that just around this bend, the hill begins to drop again and before the drop is Namita Aunty's house.

Then there it is. On my left. The line of tall eucalyptus trees. The ornamental metal fence curving around their boundary. The wooden signpost saying 'Kunnin mukaḷil' along with Aunty's full name, and the cute picture of a hilltop – lovingly painted by Nallavan Uncle before his death.

"Stop!" I call out in Malayalam.

Jintu pulls up outside the front gate.

I climb out of the auto and stretch my arms behind my head, taking in my surroundings.

Jintu sticks his head out of the auto and speaks in English. "I wait. You see family here."

I shrug. Despite the heat, a shiver of anticipation runs down my spine. It's just gone 11am so I'm not expecting anyone to be home, but I can hope. I put my hand inside the gate to pull up the latch. It's unlocked. Dragging back the gate, I step through and trip my way across the paved yard. Beautiful bougainvillea plants are in clumps on either side of the front door. The house itself is a large two-storey house with faded pink walls. I climb up the granite porch steps and notice that the door is wide open. Dry mouthed, I stand at the door and call out, "Hello... is anyone home?"

"One moment!" a male voice calls back. There's the sound of a flush, and a few seconds later, a tall bespectacled young man comes out of the downstairs bathroom drying his hands on his trousers. It's my cousin Abhishek. He's filled out – in a good way – and is far less lanky than when I last saw him in person.

He stares at me and his mouth drops open. "Oh my god. Sathya, no? What are you doing here?"

I shrug again, trying to act nonchalant. It's Abhishek, after all. If it was one of the girls, I might have shown a bit more emotion. I certainly feel emotional enough. It's like I've been on fast charge all morning and now I'm buzzing and ready to go, but with nowhere *to* go. "None of the usual, 'hey how are you doing, Sathya? Would you like to come in, sit down, make yourself at home.'"

Abhishek raises an eyebrow and says, "If that's what you want." He strolls across the tiled floor to the living area and plumps up the cushions on one of the sofas. "Here, come and sit down, your majesty," he says with grave affectation.

"You goof," I say with a laugh. "Hey, I'd better just go and tell my driver that there's someone home so he can leave."

"You came by auto? I'll talk to him – you get yourself comfortable," he says walking past me out the door grinning.

Taking off my shoes and socks, I stuff my socks inside, and pad across the floor to the sofa where I slump down, enjoying the cool from the ceiling fan. On the polished table just across from me are three large photo frames – one of the three children taken about six years ago, one of Namita Aunty and Nallavan Uncle looking very young, serious and glammed up on their wedding day, and the other of Ammamma and Muthachan. To my left near the front door is a raised shrine area with a statue of Ganesh, the elephant god, incense sticks and marigold flowers spread out around him.

My skin throbs and my fingers are enlarged and stumpy from the heat.

"So, how come you're not at uni?" I ask when Abhishek re-enters, "And where's Ammamma?"

"Wo!" Abhishek says in mock shock coming to sit on a nearby sofa. "I think you're the one who needs to answer my questions first. Anyway, questions can wait, my dear cousin. Let me get you a drink – tea, coffee, juice?"

"A tea please," I say looking forward to a proper Keralan chai, "And a glass of water."

"I'll be right with you, ma'am," he says with a deadpan face. He bows deeply and heads to the kitchen.

I giggle. I appreciate this sort of banter to keep things light otherwise I can see myself collapsing in a puddle of tears.

While Abhishek makes me a drink, I use the bathroom. A few minutes later, Abhishek hands me a cup of milky chai and puts the water down on the coffee table. "Do you want to come and see Ammamma now or shall we talk first? She's sitting on a chair in the back porch. She likes the shade and the flowers there."

"I'll come with you," I say and follow Abhishek out to the back of the house. The gentle critch critch critch of cicadas is in my ears. Ammamma turns her wrinkled, walnut-like skin to me as I come out of the house. She frowns disapprovingly. "Vidhya Mol? Those jeans don't fit your shape," she says in Malayalam, holding out her hand to me to hold. I clasp her hand tentatively.

"I'm not..." I start to say, then see Abhishek shaking his head at me. It's no use. She won't believe me, even if I tell her. "A child," I finish. I don't know the precise Malayalam words to say much more.

"You'll always be my child," Ammamma says tugging on my arm then releasing it. There's a note of wistfulness pushing through her seeming gruffness. "You go," she says with a dismissive wave of her hand, "back to whatever you young people do inside."

"You knew she had dementia, didn't you?" asks Abhishek as we sit back down. I toy with the handle on my cup and sip the chai slowly. Except for Ammamma, everyone in the family speaks fluent English.

"Of course, but I'd not seen her like this before. I don't look enough like mum for her to think I'm her, surely?" I ask rhetorically.

"She thinks I'm Achan all the time," Abhishek says matter-of-factly.

There's a lump in my throat. "Are you going to try the new gene therapy on her?"

He shakes his head. "There's no chance. She's developed it too late on in life. In India, they're reserving gene therapy for those with a history of dementia in the family – but only when they're under 70. We don't have any known cases in our family history, so we didn't pick this up before it was too late."

"Oh," I say. What else is there to say?

"By the way, you asked me earlier why I'm at home. Friday is my home study day."

"I can see you're working really hard," I goad.

"I was till you turned up. I'm taking a bachelor's in architecture in case you're interested."

I nod, then pre-empt his next question with, "I'm sure you're dying to know why I'm here, right?"

"Of course," he says running his fingers through a flop of hair.

"I was just wondering if I could wait to answer all your questions until Aunty and the girls come home? That way I don't have to go through everything twenty times," I say, giving him a wry smile.

Abhishek looks at me quizzically, opens his mouth to speak, shuts it then opens it again. I can tell he's wrestling with his curiosity. "Ok, fair enough. They'll all be home by 5:30pm. We can talk then. Until then, do you want to take some rest?"

"Well, one thing I'd really like to do is have a proper shower... It's been a while!"

"I didn't like to say anything," Abhishek says, wrinkling his nose at me. "But seeing as you've mentioned it..."

I give him a playful thwack on the side of his head. "You try hiding on a boat for two weeks and see how fresh you smell!"

"Aha – now you're giving me something," he says. "A little bit of winding up and it's all coming out."

"That's all you're getting – for now," I say, compressing my lips. "I'm going to leave you in peace while I go and freshen up."

"Sathya Mol!" Namita Aunty's bracelets jangle as she flings her arms around me, squeezes me against her large chest and kisses me over and over. She smells like coconut oil. "Your mother has been so worried about you – and here you are in my house, safe and alive. Thank God! What are you doing here, my child? What has happened to you?"

I can see that my hope of sharing everything in one neat go to the whole family is not going to happen. Whether I like it or not, I'm going to have to start answering their questions. It's not fair on them otherwise.

I'm just telling Namita Aunty about the reality of the tolerance agenda, when petite Prasoona arrives home from school leaving a trail of sandals, bags and books on the floor as she wanders in. "Sathya Chechi!" she squeals. She was eleven last time I saw her and now she's almost a woman with her high cheekbones and ridiculously long eyelashes. "How did you get here?" she asks.

Sighing inwardly, I start my story all over again, but focus on the bits that Prasoona would understand best like the social media banning and don't try to explain all the political stuff.

Prasoona, Abhishek and Aunty are leaning forward in various poses of intrigue. Ammamma is lying in bed now, uninterested in the proceedings. I keep nibbling from a plate of onion pakoda to give my hands something to do. I'm recounting the moment Lisa duped me on the streets of Sheffield when a husky female voice calls out from the front door, "Amma, I have to tell you about my day. It was awful!" It's sixteen-year-old Nadia, the last of the cousins to arrive. She's not noticed me sitting there yet as my back is turned to her.

There's an awkward pause. Namita Aunty folds her arms and tosses her head at Nadia. "It's going to have to wait, Nadia Mol. Look who's here."

I turn around and smile at a jittery Nadia. "Oh my god..." she says in a level voice, then "Oh my god!" she repeats in a higher pitch. "We were all worried that you'd been kidnapped or something...?"

"You're not far off the mark," I say.

"Sathyaaaa! What happened??" Nadia comes and sits down next to me on the sofa and pats my cheeks affectionally.

"I can see I'll need to start all over again." I'm both weary and delighted with all the attention.

Namita Aunty takes charges. "You enlighten Nadia on the first part of the story. Abhishek, Prasoona and I will be in the kitchen. Then you can tell the rest of the story over dinner, no?"

It's 8pm by the time we've washed our hands after dinner – we always eat with our hands in Kerala – and I've told the whole story in piecemeal fashion with lots of questions, indignation and commentary thrown in.

Visibly shaking with anger, Namita Aunty gives me another – somewhat protective – hug and tells me, "No daughter of mine should be allowed to go through what you've gone through. That law that you described is a bad, bad law and should be fought against. I can't believe...." Her voice tails off.

I can guess what she wants to say, but I know she doesn't want to be disloyal to her sister and brother-in-law in front of me.

Instead, she finishes off with, "that you went through that hell. I've texted your mum already to tell her you're safe. You can use my phone to give her a holographic call. She's doing a night shift, so you'll catch her now."

It's 2:30pm in the UK. Naomi will also be around as it's a Friday – a virtual school day. Dad may be in meetings, but I'd imagine he'd get out of one in order to see me.

I'm feeling sick all of a sudden. This is not going to be easy. I take a deep breath and drink some water.

"I need to be alone," I say softly to Namita Aunty.

"No problem, Molé. I'll get you set up with my phone in your room."

The air-con unit is just above my head. It is chilly so I adjust it to from 18 to 20 degrees and sit back against the wall next to my bed.

All of a sudden it hits me – how can I face my beloved family? The fact of Naomi's betrayal remains, and my parents were also complicit. The nastiest part of me wants to punish them and make them feel guilty, but I take a deep breath and push past my self-righteousness. This is my opportunity to reconnect with them, to love them.

Within seconds, the connection has been made and the

familiar shape of my mum forms in the room with me. A second later, Naomi appears too. Both have that washed-out appearance that comes from crying a lot. All my thoughts of punishment are gone. They've suffered enough.

"Sathya Mol, we thought you were dead!" Mum says. "And here you are, alive in front of us!"

"Yes," I say. I can't speak more since my throat has tightened at the sight of their tearful faces.

"Where's Dad?" I finally ask.

"He's in an important meeting. He passes on his love. He'll catch up with you as soon as he can," Mum says, like I need convincing of my Dad's love.

"Whatever you do," I begin, "please don't say, 'I told you so.'" Despite the coolness of the surrounding air, my head is throbbing. I can't stand this. I don't want any smugness from them regarding their warnings to me.

Naomi and Mum give one another a knowing glance. Naomi turns to me and says, "Not a chance, Sathya. We're so, so sorry about the way things have gone. Since you disappeared, I left the T-team – I couldn't bear to be part of it anymore. It felt so wrong. Can you forgive me, Sathya?"

Naomi's voice snags, her eyes fill again and within seconds, we're all bawling our eyes out. It's a snotty, eye-blurring mess, but so healing.

With a final shudder and a blowing of my nose, I say, "Of course I forgive you, Naomi and you, too, Mum, for your part."

"I just wanted the best for you," Mum says, sniffling. "I didn't want to see your life go down the drainpipe."

"Please tell Mayeso and Taila I'm safe too," I say. I can't confront my mum's attitude right now. I just need to get through this. "I've not had access to a phone for several weeks now – or when I have it's not been safe to do so. I'm sure that I can get my own phone here now though." I pause to gather my thoughts. There are so many unanswered questions. "Do you know what happened to me?"

"Not exactly," says Naomi. "Nobody told us anything..."

Mum interrupts, "The police were downright obstructive!"

Naomi grimaces. "But we figured out that it was some sort of state sponsored 'disappearance' based on what we did know."

"When are you coming home?" Mum asks, holding out her hand to me.

"I can't," I say. "I'm on the run from a mind-control centre. It's not safe. I'm planning to claim asylum here."

"My child – an asylum seeker – when she has a perfectly good home here!" Mum wails. She's so full of contradictions; I'll never fully understand her.

"It's better than a dead or mind-sapped child," I snap at her, then sigh. "Sorry for snapping, Mum, but *please* try to understand. It's a long story. You've got time, right?"

"Of course," Mum and Naomi say in unison.

We're on the call for well over an hour. At the end of it, Mum finishes by saying, "Your Aunty messaged me to say that we've all been blindsided to the full extent of what's going on, here. She's right," Mum says. It's hard for Mum to admit when she's been wrong about something so this is a poignant moment for me. "The truth is, I don't know what we can do about it." She sniffles again. "It's so engrained in our culture now."

"I don't know either," I respond. Then somehow I do. "I guess it's in the small resistances to an evil agenda that masquerades as something good. Only you can figure out what that means for you."

"We'll have a think and a chat about it," says Naomi. "I've

got to go now," she says, "I've got a history assignment that's due soon. That's one thing that you've wangled your way out of!" she says wryly.

"Ha, like that was my main aim!"

"Love you, big sister," Naomi says fondly. She always calls me big sister when she really wants to show me affection. I'm something like two minutes older than her!

"Love you too, nimbycheeks," I respond.

"Hey, watch it!" Naomi chides, before Mum and her shimmer out of view.

I have downloaded the Bible onto Aunty's phone and am sitting outside on the flat roof of their house reading it. The cicadas chirp in the warm morning sunlight and bees buzz around the brightly coloured flowers in their pots.

Quiet footsteps behind me alert me that someone is nearby. I turn around and see Prasoona. She comes and sits down next to me on the ground. "I'm glad you're here with us," she says. "I'm looking forward to having you around more." Prasoona holds out her hand to me and I squeeze it.

"Me too," I say. "It's not the circumstances I would have expected, but something tells me that I'll learn more from being here than I ever would just going about my normal life in the UK."

Prasoona is quiet for a moment then squints up at me in my chair, shading her eyes against the brightness with one hand. "I'm just thinking how much Vidhya Aunty and Anthony Uncle will miss having you around, but at least you're in a safe place. Your safety is the most important thing, isn't it?"

"I suppose it is," I say, turning the thought around in my mind. Safety, security and space to be. Sometimes we don't have those things and at that time God is with us in the valley. I should know because I've been there.

Sunbeams of hope fill my soul again. I may not be on the path that I planned for myself, but God has it in hand, and I know that there are adventures afoot.

Acknowledgements

The process of writing any book, while a solitary process for the most part, is very much sharpened by other people and their insights. First of all, I want to thank my novel writer's group – Louise Wilford, Matthew Chetwood, Pavitra Menon and Chris Bullivant – for their insights into the early stages of T for Tolerance. Pavitra was also invaluable for her insights into some cultural accuracies.

Secondly, I want to thank my teen beta readers – Zoe Mileman and Abigail Haine – for their thoughts regarding the first draft of my novel from the perspective of my key audience. I also want to thank the unnamed reader of my book from Instant Apostle who gave some challenging insights – some of which I agreed with and some that I didn't – which certainly helped me sharpen the narrative. And I'm indebted to Mark Anderson Smith for his thoughtful comments on the worldbuilding aspects of my novel. Writing something set only 20 years in the future is harder than you might think!

I also want to thank Joanna Penn for her brilliant podcast and her encouragement (from a distance!) to step out into the world of self-publishing. There are countless others from the Association of Christian Writers network who have supported in various ways including giving practical advice on self-publishing, giving feedback on my cover and blurb and generally being warm, encouraging cheerleaders. You've all played a small part in the journey.

I am grateful for the AI tools I have used to aid my editing process – including ProWriting Aid and Sudowrite. While *T for Tolerance* is very much a work of my own imagination, AI has been used to improve the overall readability.

Finally, I want to thank my husband, Blessan, for being my best friend and encourager and I want to praise God for being my ultimate source and the perfect Creator.

Other books by Katherine Blessan

Full length adult novels:

Home Truths with Lady Grey (The Conrad Press, 2022)
  Lydia's Song: The story of a child lost and a woman found (Instant Apostle, 2014)

As a contributor:

Simply Eat: Everyday Stories of Friendship, Food and Faith (Instant Apostle, 2018)
  'Sayyida Nanda' in *The Word for Freedom: Short Stories of Women's Suffrage* (Retreat West Books, 2018)
  'Travels by Wheelchair' in *Refugees and Peacekeepers* (Patrician Press, 2017)

To find out more about Katherine's work and keep up with future publications, including the sequel to *T for Tolerance*, please sign up at www.katherineblessan.com or using the below QR code and scrolling to the bottom of the page.